A SEASON FOR SINGING

West Berlin—an uneasy island in a sea of
Communism; a place where people live on
their nerves. Anne Holbrook, a young
widow, lives here as secretary to novelist
Robert French and whipping-boy to his
wife, Miriam, whom Anne suspects of
having an affair with Charles Ellistone, an
official at the British Consulate. The
arrival of the Frenchs' son, Adrian, and
Robert's brother Ian, upsets the balance of
relationships in the house and precipitates
a chain of mystifying and frightening
events. Anne is trapped in the growing
web, cut off from any help by a wall which
she feels forced to keep building—a wall of
lies.

A SEASON FOR SINGING

Mary Mackie

CURLEY LARGE PRINT
HAMPTON, NEW HAMPSHIRE

Library of Congress Cataloging-in-Publication Data available

British Library Cataloguing in Publication Data available

This Large Print edition is published by Chivers Press, England, and by
Curley Large Print, an imprint of Chivers North America, 1993.

Published by arrangement with the author.

U.K. Hardcover ISBN 0 7451 1778 3
U.K. Softcover   ISBN 0 7451 1787 2
U.S. Hardcover ISBN 0 7927 1550 0
U.S. Softcover   ISBN 0 7927 1524 1

Printed in Great Britain

'Not always fall of leaf, nor ever Spring,
Not endless light, nor yet eternal day.
The saddest birds a season find to sing.
The roughest storm a calm may soon allay.'

Saint Peter's Complaint, Robert Southwell
(1561–1595)

CHAPTER ONE

Berlin, to the tourist, is a fascinating city, with its wealth of buildings, new and historic, its woods and its lakes. But to live there for any length of time is to become aware of subtle undercurrents of tension. The city's gaiety inclines towards the frantic: its people live to the limit, as if there may be no tomorrow. Berlin is an island trying hard not to sink in the surrounding sea of Communist East Germany.

At the time, after living in Berlin for eight months, I was unaware of how the insidious atmosphere was affecting myself and the people amongst whom I moved, but I see now that everything happened with a curious cockeyed logic which manifests itself nowhere else in the world.

★   ★   ★

On that first day—the first of the twelve which were to alter so many lives—I drove through the city towards the airport at Templehof, going fast along the wide arterial roads in time with the other traffic, which was always in a hurry. I was going to be late meeting the plane, which annoyed me because Adrian would expect someone

1

to be there and would be hurt by what he was bound to take as negligence.

It *was* negligence, at least on Miriam's part. Robert's preoccupation with his work I could understand, having lived with it for more than three years, but Miriam might have made the effort to meet her son. She, however, had pleaded a headache. It was unfortunate that I knew the 'headache' was plump and dapper and named Charles Ellistone.

I had left the car in the park and was sprinting towards the airport entrance when I saw Adrian emerge from the doorway and shade his eyes to look out over the parked vehicles. When I waved, he turned briefly to the tall man by his side and they both began to walk towards me.

Adrian was fifteen, with his father's height and build, which looked incongruous in the black school blazer. His hair and features, though, were pure Miriam—black hair and jutting axe-blade nose, deep-set dark eyes that could sparkle or brood without warning—but as yet he had not developed the bitterness which overlay his mother's hard countenance. I loved the boy as a brother, feeling for him when he was hurt by the disinterest of his parents and fearing that the life he led would turn him into a delinquent.

He looked pleased to see me and shifted

2

his case so that he could shake hands.

'Hello, Mrs Holbrook. Dad was too busy to come, I suppose?'

'Yes, Adrian. He was sorry, but...'

'I'm used to it,' he interrupted. 'This is my Uncle Ian, as you've probably gathered.'

My hand was enveloped in Ian French's and I had to lift my head to meet dark blue eyes that were frankly admiring. Something about the slow smile he gave me made me aware that he, too, was conscious of the immediate recognition between us—a recognition that had nothing to do with his resemblance to Robert. I withdrew my hand swiftly and turned away.

The cramped area in the back of my Kharmann Ghia wasn't really intended for a seat, but Adrian somehow squeezed himself into it and leaned on the back of the passenger seat, pointing out the landmarks to his uncle.

'That's the remains of the Kaiser Wilhelm Church,' he said as I negotiated the crowded Kurfurstendamm, where the ruined building stood between the octagonal new church and its separate tower, their walls a mass of square blue windows. 'They call the new church and tower the Compact and Lipstick. You can see why. You'll have to come down at night, Ian. It's marvellous when it's lit up from inside, isn't it, Mrs Holbrook?'

3

'It certainly is,' I agreed. 'I'm sure your uncle will enjoy seeing the city by night.' The words sounded prim and stilted, bringing a gleam of amusement into the blue eyes of the man beside me.

Adrian asked, 'How long are you staying, Ian?'

'About six months.'

'Ian's an electrical engineer, you know,' Adrian informed me. 'He's come to work in Berlin on an exchange.'

'Yes, I know.' Briefly again I glanced at Ian French, annoyed that his laconic presence should so easily shatter my tranquillity. Judging by his expression, he was amusedly aware that he had me twitching.

I drove to Kladow by the perimeter road, so that Adrian might show his uncle the watch-towers behind the barbed-wire barricade. In places, between the trees, the ploughed area beyond the fence was visible, its corrugated brown giving no indication of the mines beneath the apparently innocent surface.

'There's the biggest watch-tower, among those trees,' Adrian said with enthusiasm, leaning across his uncle's shoulder to wave at the East German soldiers who were plainly visible at the top of the tower.

I was pleased when Ian French reprimanded the boy, telling him that this

4

was not one of his school games. The proximity of enemies might be exciting to a fifteen-year-old, but I was only too aware of how easily an unpleasant incident might occur. The *Volkspolizei* were armed with high-powered rifles and their tempers were notoriously short.

The fields through which we were passing gave way to half-hidden houses and villas as we entered the popular lakeside resort of Kladow. Holidaymakers strolled beneath the trees along the winding roads which led down to Lake Havel and tents and caravans made a bright splash among the trees by the shore.

Off the main thoroughfare, the road became little more than a track, with stones filling the pot-holes. This road gave access to lakeside houses and within seconds I was turning into the driveway which fronted the big, white-painted house where window-boxes overflowed with red geraniums.

Miriam was at the door and came down the steps as the car drew up, her lips curved into a brilliant smile. As soon as Ian French was out of the car Adrian leapt after him, to be given a swift peck on the cheek before his mother turned to the tall fair man behind him.

'It's lovely to see you again, Ian,' she purred. 'At last I shall I have someone civilised to talk to.' She glanced at me, her

5

tone becoming that of mistress to servant. 'Leave the car here, Anne. We can bring the cases in after we've eaten.'

I reached the hall in time to see Robert coming down the stairs to shake hands with his brother and his son. His bulky frame was bent about the shoulders and the perpetual far-away look was there in his faded blue eyes.

'How goes it, Adrian?' he inquired with forced heartiness.

'School?' said Adrian. 'Oh, it's okay. Do you want to see my report?'

'Yes, son. But later, if you don't mind ... Good to see you, Ian. Good journey?'

'Fine,' Ian French assured him.

Miriam had gone into the dining-room and now called us in for tea.

'Anne and I will have ours in the study,' Robert said. 'Ask Eleonore to bring it up.'

'But, Dad,' Adrian protested, 'can't it wait? I've got a lot to tell you...'

Emerging from the dining-room, Miriam placed a possessive arm around her son's shoulders, saying, 'You know your father's work is the most important thing. His muse is working overtime and he doesn't want to leave it. Come, darling, you can tell *me* all your news.'

The bleakness I had noted at the airport returned to Adrian's eyes as he turned away from Robert. I looked hopefully at my employer, but he was already deep in his thoughts as he turned back to the stairs.

The first-floor study, as usual, needed a thorough cleaning. There were scraps of paper and cigarette ash on the carpet all round Robert's desk and the long sideboard against the wall was covered by a jumble of oddments and a film of dust. Robert kept the room locked when he was not working and the German housekeeper was allowed in for only an hour every Saturday.

Robert stood in his favourite place at the balcony door, jotting notes on a pad and not bothering to glance round when the housekeeper arrived bearing our meal-tray.

Eleonore tiptoed in and placed the tray on my desk, nodding towards Robert and smiling indulgently. A small, thin woman, she was dressed all in black as usual. I nodded back and smiled, one finger to my lips.

As I began to pour the tea, Robert suddenly turned, saying, 'Good, that's done.' He came across the room and accepted a cup of tea, stirring it absent-mindedly—he didn't take sugar. 'Now we can get on with the next chapter. How are you doing?'

'I've almost caught up with you.'

'Good girl.' He strode to his desk, slopping tea into his saucer, and sat down to sharpen a pencil which already had a needle-like point.

'Robert ...' I said tentatively.

He looked up, smiling. 'Yes?'

'Can't you leave it now?' I asked. 'Surely you could take the evening off and start fresh in the morning?'

He stared at me as if I had lost my reason. 'But you know how it is with me, Anne. I can't write to order. I have to work as the mood takes me.'

'But Adrian has just arrived from school,' I pointed out. 'He has a lot he wants to tell you and he was terribly disappointed when you weren't at the airport.'

Robert reached for a cigarette and lit it before saying, 'He's got his mother and Ian to talk to. I'll be able to spend some time with him during his holidays, but tonight ... no, I'm sorry. I must carry on. You can go down when you've finished what you're doing.'

He bent over the loose-leaf file he used for writing in long-hand, his mind already far away, and I knew that it would be useless to argue with him.

★   ★   ★

In the lounge, the sun's rays were slanting through the open french windows on to the red brocade settee, where Miriam and Adrian were looking at the boy's school report. Ian French stood before the huge German-style dresser, whose shallow cupboards and shelves ran the length of one wall. As I went in, Ian turned with a fat, elaborately shaped candle in his hand and asked through teeth clenched on a black briar pipe:

'Do they actually burn these beautiful things?'

'Oh, yes,' Adrian replied, strolling across to take the candle from his uncle. 'Over Christmas and birthdays and such. It's a tradition, isn't it, Mrs Holbrook?'

'Only with the smaller candles,' I said. 'It's supposed to be bad luck if they aren't burnt out by the end of the special day.'

'Seems a pity,' Ian said, taking the candle from Adrian and replacing it on the shelf.

The boy walked down the room and to another shelf, where he picked up a Dresden doll in an intricate pink dress.

'This is new, isn't it, mother?' he asked.

Miriam looked up from the school report, jumping to her feet angrily and snatching the doll from Adrian.

'You know I don't allow anyone to touch those things,' she said in a low voice, carefully returning the doll to its place. 'Leave it alone. I won't have you meddling. If you're trying to distract my attention from that shocking report, you aren't succeeding. I have never read anything so disgraceful.

9

What do you think you go to school for? You certainly don't seem to learn anything.' She went back to the settee and picked up the report, reading from it. 'Could try harder ... Seems to have no interest.' Her green eyes flashed as she glanced across at Adrian. 'Wait till your father sees this, my boy.'

Adrian shrugged. 'He'll just glance at it, smile vaguely, and tell me to do better next time. He always does.'

There was a sizzling silence, into which the doorbell rang. Glancing beyond the net curtains at the front window, I saw Charles Ellistone's car on the driveway. Miriam, too, had noted it.

'We'll talk about this later,' she said heavily. 'Just say hello to Charles and then get out of my sight.'

As she slammed the door behind her, Ian asked mildly, 'Who's Charles?'

Adrian sent him a scornful glance. 'Mother's boyfriend,' he said, and turned on his heel to stride out through the french windows.

His uncle turned astonished blue eyes on me, but I walked quickly past him to the patio, from where I saw Adrian going down the lawn and through the shrubbery to the beach.

'Who is Charles?' Ian French repeated, his deep voice from from immediately behind me.

I turned, looking up into his quizzical eyes. 'He's an Englishman who works at the Consulate. He's a friend of Robert's.'

One of his eyebrows raised sardonically. 'And is he also a friend of Miriam's?'

I looked away to avoid his searching gaze as I was forced into telling less than the truth. 'Of course. He's a friend of the whole family.'

'Then where did Adrian get the idea...?'

'I don't know,' I said quickly. 'He's a very imaginative boy. I think he said it to shock you.'

'Do you indeed?' He puffed thoughtfully at his pipe. 'And why should he want to shock me?'

I was saved from having to reply by the opening of the sitting-room door.

'Ian, my dear,' Miriam said brightly, holding out a hand. 'Do come and meet Charles Ellistone. Charles, this is Robert's brother.'

Charles Ellistone smiled charmingly and held out a pudgy hand which was shaken perfunctorily by Ian. Neatly dressed in a light grey suit, his dark hair slicked back from a round pink face adorned by a thin moustache, Charles was in his late forties and fancied himself as a ladies' man.

'My dear chap,' he enthused. 'Delighted to meet you. Heard such a lot about you.

11

Electrical engineer, I believe? Never been much good with my hands myself. More of an office bod.'

Miriam fussed around them. 'Do sit down, both of you. How about a drink? Ian, will you have a beer or ...' She broke off, glancing to where I stood on the patio. 'Where's Adrian?'

'He went for a walk,' I replied.

'Oh. Then he's all right. Are you joining us?'

'I think I'll get some air.'

Miriam's relief was obvious as she rang the bell to summon Eleonore—she was always happier when I was absent.

As I went slowly down the path, the gardener, Wilhelm, a scruffy man smoking a cheroot, appeared from the shed at the edge of the shrubbery, peeling off his dirty gloves and showing his yellow teeth in a grin.

'You're working late,' I observed.

Wilhelm shrugged hugely, spreading expressive hands, his eyes wide with non-comprehension. *'Bitte?'*

I tapped my watch. 'Late ... oh, never mind. *Guten abend.'*

He grinned again. *'Wiedersehen.'*

Adrian was sitting on a tree-stump, throwing stones into the lake. My footsteps crunched on the stony beach as I approached and in amongst the trees, where the air was busy with mosquitoes, twigs

12

cracked beneath my feet. But the boy didn't look up. He continued to fling his arm out and watch the stones plop in the water.

'Would you like to come for a walk?' I asked.

Still he kept up the stone-throwing. 'I knew it would be you,' he said. 'You're the only one who cares enough.'

'Oh, Adrian, that isn't true,' I said softly. 'Your parents both care about you.'

He bent over, scratching for more stones. 'They're both too busy with their own affairs.' He laughed bitterly. 'That's the right word, isn't it? Affairs? Especially for my mother.'

'Adrian,' I said anxiously. 'Where have you got that idea? Your mother and Charles...'

He turned on me viciously. 'I saw him kissing her, when I came at Easter. He gave her that doll. That's why I picked it up—to see what she would do.'

'You may have seen them together, but friends do sometimes kiss each other.'

The glance he gave me was full of cynicism. 'Friends! That's what the film stars say—just good friends—but everyone knows what it means.'

There was nothing I could think of to say to that, so I changed the subject and suggested we walk as far as the *wurst* stall on the lakeside.

Adrian flung a final stone into the water and drew himself to his feet, hands thrust deep into his pockets and feet kicking the pebbles as we walked. Beside him, I felt very small and very old.

The sun had gone and night was closing in. Along the lake-front at Kladow the people strolled beneath strings of coloured lights. Adrian and I joined the leaners on the railing, gazing out across the water where lights danced on the ripples. In the middle of the lake a brightly lit steamer moved, laughter and music spilling from it to float on the still night air to the shore, while on the far side of the Havel a red light glowed from the top of a radio mast like some non-conformist star.

Adrian's bitterness seemed to disperse as we stood there, and he turned to me like a small boy, asking eagerly, 'Can we have a *bockwurst*?'

We walked across the road to join the group of people standing by the stall, eating their sausages amid savoury aromas. The *bockwurst*, served on a cardboard plate with a splotch of French mustard, and eaten with a plastic fork, were appetising in the open air.

Adrian grinned down at me in the light from the stall. 'You're my favourite girl, Mrs Holbrook. We do have some fun, don't we? Remember the zoo at Easter, when you

14

tried to get me away from those monkeys with huge red behinds? I only stayed there to annoy you.'

I laughed. 'I know that, you horror.'

'I like you,' Adrian said seriously. 'You don't talk down to me the way Mother does, and Dad hardly ever talks to me at all.'

'He's so busy, Adrian. Do try to understand. He's awfully fond of you, but he gets wrapped up in his work.'

'I do understand, in a way. But I never seem to see him. The other chaps' fathers take them out during the vac. A couple of them were going to Greece this year. It's ages since we had a holiday.'

He was silent again as we returned along the beach and in the garden he paused, staring into the sitting-room, which was lit by a standard lamp near the french windows. The sound of one of Miriam's jazz records floated out to us. Robert had joined the other three and they were all sitting round a table laden with bottles and glasses, while cigarette smoke whirled in thick curls to ribbon out through the doors and lose itself on the evening breeze.

Adrian, seeming reluctant to speak to anyone else, asked if he might go upstairs through my room, and I watched as he went soundlessly up the wooden steps that led from the garage to the first-floor veranda.

My room was built above the garage and had a door on the veranda. Waiting until Adrian was inside, I squared my shoulders and advanced on to the patio.

Miriam was talking to Ian, her dark head close to his fair one as they laughed together, but when she saw me the laughter died from her face and was replaced by a dark veil of dislike.

The smoke in the room made my eyes smart and the jazz rhythm beat mercilessly at my aching head. I tried to refuse the drink that Robert offered me, but he was adamant and I was forced to join them, thinking that there were times when Robert was as sensitive as a steam-roller.

'It's turning cooler,' Robert observed, moving to close the doors. 'Look at the mosquitoes round the light.'

Standing up abruptly, Miriam went irritably to the window, taking a spray from behind the curtain and proceeding to attack the hovering insects with it, an operation which afforded Robert some amusement.

'Miriam can't bear the mozzies, can you, my love? She comes up in great red lumps when they bite her. She goes mad itching.'

Frowning, Miriam scratched at her forearm. 'Just talking about it makes me itch.'

'They don't bother me overmuch,' Charles remarked placidly. 'Must have bad

16

blood.'

Robert put an arm about his wife, who stiffened visibly at his touch. He said mockingly, 'It's bad blood they like, isn't it, my love?'

Miriam twitched away from him, then, realising that attention was focused upon her, she forced a laugh. 'You're probably right, dear.'

Charles thumped his empty glass down, rose, and stretched himself to his full five feet six. 'I must be going. Heavy day tomorrow. Have to keep to office hours, you know.'

Goodnights were said and Robert went to see Charles out.

'Where's Adrian?' Ian asked of me. 'Did you find him?'

I looked across at him. 'Yes. We went for a walk together. He's gone to bed.'

'I don't know what's wrong with that boy,' Miriam said, scratching absent-mindedly at her leg. 'He's never happy.'

'He's growing up fast,' Ian said. 'It's a difficult time for a boy. I can still remember how I felt.'

Miriam laughed, letting her hand rest on his knee and gazing into his eyes. 'I should think so, too. Wait till you're my age. Youth seems a long way away when you're growing old.'

'You aren't old,' Ian said gallantly,

accepting the bait.

Laughing softly, Miriam leaned towards him. 'Dear Ian. You're very good for my ego.'

The door opened again and Robert looked round long enough to announce that he was going back to work and Miriam needn't wait up for him as he would probably sleep on the couch in the study. As he closed the door again, Miriam turned, with a curl of the lips, to Ian.

'Think yourself honoured that he showed his face at all this evening. I hardly ever see him when he's working, which is all the time.' She drained her glass and stood up, smoothing her dress over flat stomach and hips before walking to the corner by the front window to switch off the record player. 'If you don't mind, I'll go upstairs. There's a lot to do for the dinner party tomorrow. I hope you'll be available to help me, Anne, if you can spare the time from Robert's precious book.'

'Of course, Mrs French,' I said quietly.

As soon as we were alone, Ian gave me a cigarette and lit it for me before turning his attention to his pipe.

'Is it always like this?' he asked from behind clouds of smoke.

'Like what?'

'This house feels like volcano that may erupt at any moment. Don't you feel it?'

'One gets used to it,' I said quietly.

He leaned forward, elbows on his knees. 'I can't see where you fit in. You seem out of place, somehow.'

'I work for Robert. I live in the house but I'm not really part of the family, if that's what you mean. I try to stay in the background as much as possible.'

'So I noticed. Why does Miriam dislike you?'

Since Miriam took no trouble to hide her feelings for me, this question was hardly surprising. I tried to answer honestly, though even I did not know the true reasons behind Miriam's hostility.

'I think she objects to my being close to Robert, although she must know there's nothing irregular between us. But Miriam is a very possessive woman. You must know that.'

Ian sucked on his pipe, eyes narrowed, saying after a long moment, 'They've never been really happy together. I often wonder why my brother married her at all.'

'They probably drifted into marriage, the way most people do,' I said, voicing an opinion formed by bitter experience. 'An awful lot is written about love, but who ever really finds it? It's all a great practical joke—this moonlight and roses thing. We're led to believe it happens, but it never does.'

Ian was staring at me, his blue eyes wide

19

with amazement. I had shocked him, I saw.

'That's a terrible, disillusioned attitude for one so young. Was your own marriage unhappy?'

I was annoyed now, annoyed that a stranger should dare to ask so many personal questions. 'That's right,' I said harshly. 'I was conned into it by all the guff they print in books and magazines. I was nineteen, starry-eyed and thinking the happy ending was inevitable. I soon saw how wrong I was—that it was all a trap. If Nigel hadn't been killed I might still be his wife and wondering how I ever got myself into such a mess. Or I'd be divorced and chasing other moonbeams ... But I saw the truth and now I've stopped looking for love. I don't believe there is such a thing.'

'Use your eyes,' Ian said brusquely. 'Just because you live in a house where love has no place it doesn't mean that it doesn't exist. Millions of people are happy together.'

'Out of habit,' I said scathingly. 'They're used to being together, that's all. Time wears down their resistance and they don't even realise they've been cheated.' I stubbed out my half-smoked cigarette angrily and stood up. 'I'm sure we needn't continue this conversation.'

He leaned back in his chair, half closing his eyes and remarking, as if to himself,

'You prefer to lose yourself in the dream-world which Robert creates. You're running away from reality because you've been hurt.' He raised his eyes slowly to meet mine. 'Am I right?'

'Goodnight, Mr French,' I said in a low voice, making for the door.

★   ★   ★

In my own room above the garage I unpinned my long brown hair before the mirror, brushing it out with sharp strokes, which proved how much Ian French had disturbed me. As a total stranger, he had no right to criticize my attitude to life. He was smug, self-satisfied, complacent...

As I slipped into bed I turned out the light and almost immediately was startled upright by a movement outside my veranda door, just the suggestion of a shadow on the curtain. My heart thudding, I crossed the room and drew back the curtains to see an almost full moon riding high in the sky and the trees sighing in the night wind. A movement in the garden caught my eye, but was gone when I focused on the spot. I felt the hairs on my nape prickle and my skin turn to gooseflesh; then I realized that Robert, or Ian, might have decided to take a walk.

Light spilled across the veranda from the

21

study next door and I dropped the curtain back into place, where it moved slightly in the breeze. Clearly I was imagining things.

CHAPTER TWO

The following morning I found Adrian down at the lake, wearing only a pair of shorts as he paddled in the water.

'Why don't you come and join me?' he invited.

'I'm not on holiday, unfortunately,' I laughed, 'though it does look tempting. Have you had breakfast?'

He nodded his dark head. 'Ages ago. Are you going to be busy today?'

'I'm afraid so. I've some work to do for your father and your mother asked me if I would help prepare for the dinner party tonight.'

'Dinner party? Oh, no! Who's coming?'

'Don't look so glum,' I chided. 'As a matter of fact, your father has invited Heidi Decker and...'

'The film star?' Adrian breathed, hazel eyes round with awe.

I nodded, amused by his sudden enthusiasm.

'Gosh!' he exclaimed. 'Heidi Decker! She was in that film that Dad wrote, wasn't she?

22

She's not much older than me, either.'

'She lives in that new pink villa along the shore,' I told him, pointing.

'Gosh!' he said again. 'Have you met her? What's she like?'

'Very pretty, and much the same as any other teenager. She's only eighteen—so I'm afraid her mother will be coming with her.'

Adrian glared at me. 'You don't think I actually like her, do you? It will be something to tell the boys at school, that's all.' He turned away as his uncle came down the path.

'Hey, Ian, did you know we're having a film star for dinner?'

'I hope she'll be succulent,' Ian remarked dryly, ducking as Adrian kicked water towards him.

'You know what I mean,' the boy said.

Ian grinned. 'Your mother told me. But I'm afraid I shall be rather out of my depth. The guests sound awe-inspiring.'

'Why? Who else is coming?' Adrian turned to me, groaning. 'Don't tell me ... Captain Smith and his wife: *Oberkommissar* Bracke from next door...'

'Who?' Ian asked, an expression of mock alarm on his face.

'*Oberkommissar* Bracke. He's some kind of police chief. He lives in that house next door.'

'Sounds terrifying,' Ian said feelingly.

23

Adrian bent to pick up a handful of stones and fling them far out into the Havel. 'Why does mother always have these people to dinner when I'm at home? I get so bored...'

'You're forgetting Heidi Decker,' I reminded him.

'Oh, yes. That was a brilliant idea of somebody's. I may just manage to stay awake—if I get the chance to talk to her.'

Miriam's voice came clearly to us, calling my name as she came down the path. Her dark hair was drawn tightly into a bun, giving no relief to her sharp features.

'Anne,' she said again, pausing at the edge of the beach. 'I'm going shopping for the food for the party and I want you to come. Adrian, darling, why don't you come with us?'

'I'm all right,' Adrian muttered. 'Anyway, I hate shopping.'

'Do come out of the water. You're not a child now—paddling at your age. And for goodness sake, put a shirt on.'

The boy walked into the water, ignoring his mother.

'Could I come shopping?' Ian asked unexpectedly. 'I can carry the baskets for you.'

Miriam's face lit into a delighted smile. 'Oh yes, do come. We can have lunch in town, if you like, then you can bring the

24

shopping back, Anne, and help Eleonore while I have my hair done. Adrian! ... Adrian! ... Oh, you're impossible.'

She turned and went back into the house. As Ian and I followed more slowly we saw her speaking to Eleonore, who was polishing furniture in the sitting-room.

'Looks as though Eleonore's getting her orders for the day,' Ian observed. 'Let's not disturb them. Can we go through the kitchen? Do you think I should put a jacket on if we're going to town?'

'I should put a tie on, too,' I advised, 'unless you want to be stared at.'

'Really? Oh, well ...' He buttoned his shirt, sighing. 'I suppose I'd better conform. Don't want to upset Miriam.'

Going out by the front door, I paused by the lounge window, where the window box was bright with scarlet geraniums. Inside, on the window sill, green foliage from many spreading plants helped the net curtains to screen the light and Eleonore was a busy, shadowy figure inside the room.

'Shall I be presentable like this?' Ian asked as he came from the house with Miriam.

I raised my eyebrows, as if considering his brown jacket and green tie. 'Yes, I think you'll do.'

We both laughed at this small private joke and Miriam, opening the garage doors, turned with an exclamation of annoyance.

'Are you two coming?'

She took the driver's seat in Robert's Mercedes and Ian sat beside her. We used the road through Kladow village and on past Gatow Airfield and woods and fields to Gatow village, coming out on to the wide Heerstrasse, the six-lane road that ran straight to the heart of the city. Ian expressed his surprise at finding Berlin such a pleasant place of trees and lakes, when he had expected piles of rubble.

We parked on the bustling Kurfurstendamm and walked through the back streets to the market square, which might have been an English one but for the *wurst* stalls every few yards. There was the inevitable pushing and crowding, made worse by the Germans' refusal to queue.

Miriam was a fussy shopper, poking and squeezing among the fruit and vegetables, but soon Ian was laden with three heavy baskets. We left this first load at the car and went on to the shops, where it seemed to me we visited every floor and traversed all the escalators in Miriam's search for 'just the right thing. I'm not being fobbed off with something I don't want.'

Eventually, to my relief, Miriam announced that the last item had been bought. The boot of the Mercedes was almost full when I finally slammed the lid

26

down, heaving a sigh and brushing a stray strand of hair from my forehead. I felt hot and sticky, whereas Miriam looked cool and calm. Noticing this, she smiled spitefully and tucked her hand beneath Ian's arm.

'Now, where shall we go for lunch?' she enquired.

'Didn't you say there was a restaurant on that Eiffel Tower affair?' Ian asked.

Miriam preened herself beneath his eyes. 'Oh, you will have to be educated, my dear ignoramus. That's the *Funkturm. Funk ... turm!*' She glanced at me. 'Would you rather go home? You look exhausted.'

Before I could reply, Ian had swung round to catch my elbow in his big hand, his expression daring me to leave them.

'She can do with a good meal. We'll all go together, and it's my treat.'

Miriam parked the big grey car on Hammerskjold Platz and we walked through the entrance to the Exhibition grounds which surround the metalwork tower. As we approached the long line of people waiting for the lift to take them to the very top to see the view, a familiar voice hailed us and Charles Ellistone came hurrying across the lawns, puffing a little.

'Hello, there. Going for lunch?'

'Charles, dear!' Miriam exclaimed with evident pleasure. 'How fortunate. Yes, do join us. We'll walk up, shall we?' She took

27

Charles's arm and they proceeded ahead of us.

Ian glanced down at me, remarking quietly, 'There's a coincidence!'

Ian glanced down at me, remarking quietly, 'There's a coincidence!'

'It could be just that,' I said.

A wry smile twisted his mouth. 'It could be, but we both have our doubts, don't we?'

A little out of breath, we reached the restaurant. Miriam and Charles had found a vacant table by the outward-sloping windows facing east and Miriam waved a hand irritably as Ian and I appeared.

'Where have you two been?' she demanded. 'Come along, or we'll never get served.'

Ian took one look at the menu and handed it to me, explaining that his knowledge of German was limited to electrical technicalities. Hearing this, Charles donned a pair of horn-rimmed spectacles and opened his own menu with an air of authority.

'How about some *Eisbein*?'

Miriam shuddered. 'No, thank you. Haven't they got any steak, Charles?'

Charles ran a chubby finger down the list. 'What do you say to *Kotelett mit Mischgemüse*?'

A sigh escaped Miriam's tight lips. 'Charles, dear, we know you understand it

28

and you're terribly clever, but what does it mean in plain English?'

'Sorry, my dear.' He placed a hand smilingly over hers. 'Cutlet and mixed veg.'

As soon as the meal was finished, Charles had to hurry back to the Consulate. Miriam went with him, to her hairdresser's appointment, while Ian and I sat smoking over coffee.

'Are they having an affair?' Ian asked in the blunt manner I was coming to accept as part of him.

'I don't know,' I said, looking beyond him.

'You can make an intelligent guess, can't you?' he said roughly.

I glared at him, my face hot. 'It's none of my business. You know as much as I do.'

'And Robert?'

'Robert knows they see a lot of each other. He thinks nothing of it. Why should I?'

Ian stared at me thoughtfully, removing the pipe from his mouth. 'Either he's so wrapped up in his work that he can't see what's happening, or he sees and doesn't care. Which is it?'

'How do I know? Why do you keep asking me these things?'

'You're the only one I can ask. Do you think I like to see this happening to Adrian?'

'Adrian?' I said, surprised.

29

'My own parents were divorced when I was his age. It was a shattering experience and I don't want history to repeat itself. Adrian is quite mixed-up enough already.'

'And what about Robert?'

Ian made an impatient gesture. 'Robert's old enough to take care of himself. It's his son I'm concerned about. Damn it, I thought you were concerned about him, too.'

'I am,' I protested.

'Then help me sort this thing out.'

'How? What can we do? Stop Charles from seeing Miriam? Tell Robert about it?'

'Get him to leave Berlin. God knows why he came here in the first place.'

I laughed sharply. 'He won't leave—not until the book is finished, anyway. And if he did, Miriam would find someone else. She finds it easy to charm men, as you yourself must know.'

He glowered at me, his face dark with anger. 'If you're trying to say I find her attractive you have a very poor view of me. I've always tried to be pleasant to her for Robert's sake and now that I've accepted her hospitality I have no choice but to continue being pleasant.'

I looked down at my coffee, stirring it slowly. 'You don't need to justify yourself to me. I didn't mean to imply anything.'

'Well, I'm sorry,' he said hastily. 'Drink

your coffee and let's get back.'

We walked in silence to the car and Ian waited until I had unlocked the passenger door before sliding in beside me.

'I did say I was sorry,' he said. 'I didn't mean to upset you.'

'What makes you think you have the power to upset me?' I returned tartly, twisting the ignition key with unnecessary vigour.

There was a moment's silence, then Ian said quietly, 'You poor girl. You're prickly as a hedgehog.'

I glanced at him, furious. 'I don't need your pity, either, Mr French.'

'I know,' he said complacently. 'What you need is something very different.'

I jerked the gears into reverse to back out of the parking space before pointing the car towards Kladow, driving in an angry silence prompted by conflicting emotions. What was it about this man that had the power to set me on edge? Why didn't he leave me alone? I was finished for ever with emotional entanglements.

When we reached the house I was still annoyed and slammed the car door, causing two squabbling sparrows to fly from the front lawn. Ian raised an eyebrow at me across the roof of the car.

'Are you still angry with me?'

Biting back the retort that rose to my lips,

31

I jerked the boot open and dragged one of the baskets out so carelessly that a bag of tomatoes fell on to the gravel. As I bent to retrieve the fruit, Ian came to help me, trying to hide a smile that served to make me more furious.

'I'll bring the shopping in,' he said pleasantly. 'Don't want you to strain yourself, do we?'

I brushed at my skirt, muttering, 'Thank you,' and ran up the steps to the front door, which banged back into the rubber plant as I flung it open. Eleonore, on her knees applying red polish to the tiles, looked up in astonishment.

'Do you want these in the kitchen?' Ian enquired as he came in with two full baskets.

Eleonore nodded, wiping her hands on her linen overall. '*Danke, Herr* French. The shopping—it makes you tired, *nicht*?'

'I never knew it could be such an expedition,' Ian grinned as he went past her into the kitchen. 'Mrs French is very hard to please.'

'Ah yes,' Eleonore said gravely. 'She tells me she is a ... perfectionist?'

Ian laughed, returning empty-handed. 'Is that what she calls it?' He glanced teasingly at me as he made for the front door and the rest of the shopping. 'Better now?'

I could have hit him. Instead I gave him a

look calculated to freeze. It didn't work. It only made him laugh.

★   ★   ★

I spent the afternoon in the kitchen with Eleonore and her buxom daughter Marthe, preparing food for the dinner party. The feverish activity made me forget my annoyance and when at last I was able to think about my own preparations, I was looking forward to the evening, even wondering, with the illogicality of a woman, what impression my party self would make on Ian. I told myself it was quite normal to wish to appear attractive to a male even when he meant nothing to me, but in the middle of this rationalization I left my room and met the man in question coming from the bathroom. He was wearing nothing but a towel.

'Good afternoon, Mrs Holbrook,' he said cheerfully, rubbing his curling hair with a second towel, completely unabashed by his meagre attire. 'I thought I'd have my bath before the rush starts. What time are the visitors due?'

'Eight o'clock.' I was uncomfortably aware of my frilly pink dressing gown, my sponge bag dangling from one hand, and of Ian French's massive brown frame towering beside me.

33

'I like your hair loose,' he remarked, grinning wickedly. 'It makes you look young and vulnerable—totally unlike the wildcat you really are.'

'Would you mind moving?' I said icily. 'I'd like to have a bath myself.'

He moved, smiling down at me, and I slammed the bathroom door behind me, annoyed again by my reaction to Ian's proximity.

When I emerged from the bathroom Adrian was stamping up the stairs, scowling.

'Is that bathroom free?' he demanded grumpily.

'Yes. What's the matter?'

'Oh, nothing.' He stormed on along the landing and up the stairs to the second floor as Robert looked out of the study.

My employer gazed perplexedly at his son's retreating back. 'What's wrong with him?'

'I don't know,' I replied. 'Probably been told to have a bath.'

Robert laughed. 'Most likely. Adrian and clean water are practically strangers ... You smell delicious.'

Confused, I turned away and saw Miriam standing at the top of the stairs. Her hair was curling about her neck, drawn back on one side by a diamond clip above her ear. She was wearing a tiny white apron over a dark red dress, but her glamour was spoiled

34

by the sneer on her face.

'Could you tear yourself away and come and help?' she enquired of me. 'Get dressed as quickly as you can and come to the kitchen.'

'Anne's not your servant,' Robert said loudly. 'She's been in the kitchen all afternoon. I think she deserves a rest, and enough time to get ready properly.'

'Oh,' Miriam said sweetly, 'is she joining us?'

Robert took a step forward, his hands clenching, but Miriam had gone lightly down the stairs.

'I don't mind helping,' I said. 'It won't take me long to dress.'

'You take your time,' Robert said darkly. 'She's got Eleonore and Marthe. She only wants to show she's mistress of this house ... And ignore that remark about joining us. Of course you're invited to the party.'

When I was dressed in a flowing silk gown that hugged my figure and my hair was piled in Grecian curls, I went slowly down the stairs, wondering if Miriam would make a point of objecting to my presence. Then Ian emerged from the sitting-room wearing a dinner jacket and black bow tie, and stood looking up at me with admiration warming his eyes. He held out his hand for mine as I came down the last few steps and lifted it to his lips before raising a smiling face.

'When on the Continent ...' he misquoted.

I withdrew my hand, resisting the temptation to smile back. 'They don't do that here—they only shake hands.'

'Oh, sorry, another of my *faux pas*. But you mustn't blame me. You look stunning.'

'There you are at last,' Miriam said as she came from the kitchen. 'I want you to check that the table is laid properly. And then you might see if Eleonore needs any more help. Oh, and see what's keeping Adrian and Robert. The guests will be here in fifteen minutes.' She slipped her arm through Ian's, dismissing me. 'Let us have a cocktail, Ian dear.'

The indignity of being ordered about in this manner was somewhat mitigated by the conspiratorial wink which Ian sent me over his sister-in-law's head as he was led away.

Everything in the dining-room was perfectly in order, as Miriam had no doubt known. The dark wood of the round table reflected the gleaming cutlery and twin silver candelabra with slim red candles waiting to be lit. Starched white napkins stood before each of the twelve places and, in a silver bowl at the centre of the table, a mass of red roses glowed in the evening light. I touched one of the roses, making a gesture of rearrangement to satisfy my

36

pride.

As I left the dining-room Adrian was coming down the stairs.

'Where is everyone?' he asked. 'Is my tie straight?'

I re-tied the bow for him, smiling into his anxious face. 'Quite the suave young man, Adrian. I expect you'll knock Heidi Decker sideways.'

Adrian blushed, grimacing. 'I bet she won't even notice me. I feel an awful fool dressed like this.'

'You look very nice,' I assured him. 'Do you know where your father is?'

'He was singing in the bath when I came past.'

I gasped. 'Oh, dear, your mother will have a fit. I'd better go and hurry him up.'

Robert was indeed still in the bathroom, singing *Old Father Thames* in a melodic baritone. When I knocked sharply on the door the singing stopped abruptly.

'Who's that? What do you want?'

'It's nearly eight,' I called. 'Do hurry up, Robert.'

The door opened a crack and his face appeared, grinning devilishly. 'Is Miriam going hairless?'

'You're as bad as your son!' I scolded.

Robert laughed. 'All right, woman. I'm coming.'

Still following Miriam's instructions, I

looked into the kitchen, but Eleonore insisted that there was no more for me to do. With strange reluctance, I braced myself to enter the sitting-room. Miriam, however, ignored me.

Ian was pouring me a sherry when the doorbell rang and Robert's voice from the hall told us he would answer it. The first arrivals were Captain and Mrs Smith—he tall and bespectacled, she a glamorous redhead wearing pink.

'Selena, my dear.' Miriam kissed the redhead on her averted cheek. 'And Harry ... How are you?' She glanced round at Ian, introducing him and explaining that Robert had been in the Army with Harry 'years ago'.

Selena Smith fluttered false eyelashes at Ian, her red curls dancing above a heart-shaped face that belied her age. Her husband strolled across to give Ian a firm handshake, looking more like a business man than an Army officer.

Their arrival had masked the appearance of Robert, who was wearing dark slacks and an open-necked shirt. I was unaware of his presence until Miriam said in a strangled voice, 'Robert!'

If Robert heard, he ignored her. He excused himself to answer the doorbell again.

The new arrivals were the Brackes, whom

38

Adrian had at one time described as 'that red-faced man with the broad-shouldered waist' and 'his prison-wardress wife'. This was an irreverent, but accurate description of the two people now shaking hands round the room. Frau Bracke seemed to wear nothing but grey crepe and was a timid, self-effacing person, unhelped in the present company by her lack of English. The *Oberkommissar*, however, was a forceful and deliberate speaker, wont to launch into lengthy discourse about his work with Counter Intelligence. Sometimes he could become a bore.

He came to shake hands with me, bowing as much as his stomach would allow. With his thatch of iron-grey hair and red, smiling face with wide black eyes, he reminded me of an elderly golliwog.

From his corner by the french windows, Adrian's excited voice was heard above the murmuring in the room.

'Mother! Here she comes! Her car came along the track by the beach.'

Miriam fingered her diamond necklet, looking flustered. 'Go and meet her, darling. Ask her to come straight in.'

Adrian dashed away on to the patio and down the lawn, where I could see Heidi Decker walking slowly up the path, holding her long white skirt above her ankles. One tanned young shoulder was bare and her

39

hair was a shining golden curtain falling from a centre parting. Having spoken to her, Adrian followed behind with a dazed expression on his face, while Heidi's mother, a stocky blonde woman in a navy-blue suit, bustled forward, unnecessarily holding the door back for her daughter.

Heidi stepped on to the patio and the room fell silent as everyone stopped talking to stare. The young actress paused momentarily, with the late sun behind her making a halo of her hair and showing the silhouette of lithe young legs through the floating dress, while the bushes of the shrubbery made a frame for her perfect figure.

Ian's voice whispered in my ear, 'How to make an entrance, in one easy lesson. She's not a patch on you, though.'

I kept my face averted, not wanting him to see the pleasure this outrageously untrue remark had given me.

When we were called into the dining-room, I found myself placed between Charles Ellistone and *Oberkommissar* Bracke. Miriam had arranged the places and no doubt guessed that I would be most uncomfortable between these two men. It was one of her little efforts to keep me in place. Across the table from me, Ian was flanked by Heidi Decker and Selena Smith.

He appeared to be enjoying himself tremendously.

Adrian, I was pleased to see, soon involved Heidi in conversation, so he at least was not bored, but the dinner was spoiled for me by Charles, who continually leant upon me to whisper inanities in my ear. Miriam kept up a gay flow of conversation with all her guests, though she darted disapproving glances at her informally dressed husband, who remained oblivious of her.

At the end of the meal, Robert poured brandy for everyone except Adrian, who was given more champagne. He had already had his share of wine and was alarmingly flushed. Then Robert handed round cigars and cigarettes and suggested removing to the comfort of the lounge. They eddied round me, talking and laughing as they edged through the door until only Robert and myself were left. Miriam, the last to go, paused in the doorway to tell me in a peremptory tone to fetch some ice.

Robert swore softly as his wife followed the guests.

'Robert,' I said, 'couldn't you have put a jacket and tie on?'

He frowned. 'I hate monkey jackets. Don't you worry. My friends all know me well enough not to care what I wear. It's only Miriam—she's so damn conservative.'

He must have known he was being pig-headed, but nothing I could say would change him.

In the kitchen, where I went to get the ice, Eleonore was in tears as she washed the dishes. She glanced round at me and then jerkily took up a tea-cloth and began to dry a plate.

'Eleonore,' I said, concerned. 'What is it? Has someone upset you?'

Eleonore shook her grey head. '*Nein*. No. It is ... I cannot go to see my sister when they have the opening of the Wall. She is in the East, you know. I have been at *Ostern* ... how do you say?'

'Easter?'

'*Jah*, Easter.' She wiped her eyes with a sodden handkerchief. 'So I can have not a permit for next time.'

I put an arm round her thin shoulders. 'But you'll be able to go the time after that, won't you? Don't cry, Eleonore.'

'But my sister, she is ill. I have a fright that she will die before I can go and ... oh, I am sorry, *Frau* 'olbrook, but I hear all the laughter and ... and *Frölichkeit* and I have a great sadness inside. I must go and empty the table. I am okay.'

After filling the ice-bowl, I returned to the lounge, where Robert had installed himself by the front window with Harry Smith and *Oberkommissar* Bracke. Charles sat on the

42

arm of Miriam's chair as she chatted to Selena Smith, occasionally trying to include the reticent *Frau* Bracke in the conversation, with Charles's help as interpreter. *Frau* Decker, Heidi's mother, sat with this group, but she was keeping a watchful eye on her daughter and Adrian, who were out on the patio talking to Ian amid much laughter.

As I put the ice-bowl on the cocktail cabinet, Ian was suddenly beside me, his ubiquitous pipe between his teeth.

'Where have you been?'

'Fetching the ice. Miriam asked me to.'

'You mean she ordered you. She treats you like a skivvy.'

'Well, I am an employee.'

'You're Robert's secretary, not the housemaid ... Anyway, you're here now and I'm going to see that you enjoy yourself.' He poured me a glass of champagne, presenting it with a bow. 'Adrian,' he said, 'is telling that girl about biology lessons at school. I don't think she understands half of it, but she's spellbound. I didn't get a look in.'

'Poor you,' I said sarcastically.

Ian was about to reprimand me when Miriam appeared at his elbow, begging him to come and join Selena, who was 'dying' to talk to him. With a look of mock despair, Ian was drawn away from me.

I watched Selina Smith's pert face light

into a smile as Ian sat beside her. She was showing a good deal of leg and bosom and I caught myself thinking bitchy thoughts until Harry Smith strolled across the room to the cocktail cabinet.

'I've been told to help myself,' he told me. 'Where's the Scotch? Ah. Yes. That's the stuff. And how's Mrs Holbrook? I didn't get a chance to speak to you at dinner.'

'I'm very well, thank you. And you?'

'Mustn't grumble.' He leaned against the wall, watching the other members of the party through narrowed eyes. I could not read his expression, masked as it was by his heavy glasses. His thin hand, the back of it covered by dark hairs, trembled slightly as he drew on his cigar, and I noticed that the wings of grey in his thinning dark hair were more pronounced than when I had last seen him. Did he, I wondered, worry about his flirtatious wife?

'Are you keeping busy?' I asked, making conversation.

He grimaced. 'As always, it's hectic at work. You know what it's like in Berlin—one panic after another. With my job it's always like that.'

'Oh?'

He looked sideways at me and I said quickly, 'I'm sorry. I forgot you can't talk about it. How are the children?'

Captain Smith began to tell me a tale

about his offspring and as he finished Adrian and Heidi came from the patio. The boy's eyes were overbright and his tie was on the skew.

'... and guess what happened,' he was saying. 'Old Grumbles never said a word. He just went red in the face and stormed out.'

Heidi laughed helplessly. 'I do not believe it.'

'I swear it's true,' Adrian said.

'What's all this?' Harry Smith put in. 'What are you telling her, Adrian?'

'Oh, something that happened at school. Have another drink, Heidi.'

'There's some lemonade here,' I said, hoping that Adrian would take the hint.

'We're on champers,' he replied airily, refilling his own and Heidi's glasses. I frowned at him but he ignored me, beginning to tell the anecdote of 'Old Grumbles' for Harry Smith's benefit. Having heard the story before, I slipped away to join the plump Bracke, who was temporarily alone by the front window.

'Would you like another drink, *Oberkommissar*?'

He held up his glass, which was still half full. 'Not yet, thank you, Mrs Holbrook.' His English was good but heavily accented. 'You look very charming.'

'Thank you,' I said, and after that bright

45

start the silence lengthened until Adrian and Heidi joined us, with Harry Smith hovering behind them.

'Hello, *Oberkommissar*,' Adrian greeted. 'Caught any good spies lately?'

There was an awkward pause, then Captain Smith said cheerfully, 'I saw you coming out of the C.O.'s office today. Any trouble?'

'No. No,' said the *Oberkommissar* easily. 'Merely a routine call. I have to keep an eye on things, of course.' He turned to me, saying, 'Did you know, Mrs Holbrook, there are more than a hundred thousand spies in West Berlin, more than in all the rest of the world. Every person with a relative in the East—and they are many—is a potential spy for the Communists. They write letters and send parcels. I tell you, my job is a difficult one. Anyone who visits the East may be selling information, but how can we watch everyone?' He shook his heavy head. 'Ach, it is not possible.'

Adrian looked at Heidi with a comical expression of suspicion. 'Heidi, you often work in East Berlin. Are you one of the dreaded spies?'

Amid the general laughter, I saw Bracke smile grimly to himself as he rose to his feet.

'Excuse me, please. I must see that my wife is happy. She speaks so little English ...' He brushed past Adrian and moved

46

away.

'Is that right, though?' Adrian asked. 'Over a hundred thousand spies? That must be nearly everyone in Berlin.'

'Not quite,' Smith said. 'But every other person could be involved in some way—or so we're led to believe ... Miss Decker, I saw your latest film the other day. I enjoyed it tremendously.'

Heidi lowered her eyes demurely. '*Danke*, Herr Schmidt. I think I was not good, *aber* ... dis I always tink, *naturlich*.'

'Nonsense,' Robert's voice broke in. 'You were superb, Heidi.'

Smith turned to him, saying, 'Of course, that was the film of your book—what was it? *Sighing and Singing*? Yes, I read it, but wasn't the film a bit different? Did you write the screen-play?'

Robert pulled a face. 'I did. They made me change the whole thing round, gave it another title. By the time they'd finished I hardly recognised the thing myself. Still, you can't bite the hand that feeds ... Anyone ready for another drink?'

He drifted away with Harry Smith. Adrian began telling Heidi another of his school stories and, as they seemed happy together, I withdrew, troubled by all the talk of spies. I had never given much thought to the subject before, but now I was watching everyone, remembering Harry Smith's

47

CHAPTER THREE

'Penny for them,' Ian broke into my thoughts.

'Oh ... just thinking.'

'Not very happy thoughts, either, by the look of it. What were you talking about over there?'

'Lots of things. Adrian's school. Films. Books ... and spies.'

'Spies? Yes, I suppose this city's riddled with them. Bound to be. Don't tell me you suspect someone here?'

'No, of course I don't.'

Ian turned, surveying the assembled company. 'Charles,' he said softly.

Startled, I glanced to where Charles was intently discussing something with *Frau* Decker. 'Why?'

'He works at the Consulate, doesn't he?'

'Yes, but he's only a minor cog.'

'And what about Harry Smith?' Ian went on. 'His wife was saying he's something to do with Intelligence. Anyway, it's hush-hush. And then there's Bracke—now he could be a counter-spy. Or his wife—a very sinister person.'

I had to laugh at this ridiculous

48

suggestion. 'Poor *Frau* Bracke, she wouldn't hurt a fly.'

'What's more,' Ian said, 'Robert's taking me for a trip through the Wall on Saturday. Maybe you'd better come with us, to make sure we don't pass any information.'

I noticed Harry Smith going out with the empty ice-bowl, going to the kitchen where was Eleonore, who had a sister...

'Let's change the subject,' I said hurriedly.

'All right. I'm starting work on Monday. There's an interesting piece of useless information. Will you miss me?'

'There'll be more room in the house,' I said.

Ian sighed heavily. 'Thank you kindly. It's obvious you're crazy about me. That's the trouble with me. I don't have the knack with women.'

'I wouldn't say that,' I said.

'No? Then why do you suppose I'm still a bachelor? I'm past thirty, you know.'

'I expect you prefer being single.'

'Not at all. I'm just waiting for the right woman.'

'Don't start that again,' I sighed. 'You don't really believe you'll fall madly in love and live happily ever after?'

'No. No marriage is perfect. There will be ups and downs, I expect, but at least I believe in something. What else is life for?'

'Life is for living,' I said firmly. 'Each of us lives in his own way. What you look for is your own affair. I'm not trying to change your way of thinking.'

'You couldn't. But one of these days I'm going to change yours.'

I smiled bitterly at him. 'I wish you luck. But I can tell you now it's no use.'

'The irresistible force and the immovable object,' he murmured. 'One of us is going to come the devil of a cropper.'

Miriam had left her seat and was saying something to Robert, indicating Adrian, who was still talking to Heidi. Robert strode across to them and spoke to his son, who stood up, glaring angrily with eyes wide in a flushed face.

'I'm only asking you to be sociable!' Robert's voice thundered out.

The room sang with sudden silence.

'What's the matter?' Adrian asked tauntingly. 'Are you afraid she's more interested in me than in you?'

He ducked away, sensing Robert's slight movement towards him. His elbow flew back and caught one of the shelves behind him. And the Dresden doll, Miriam's treasured gift from Charles, teetered on its small pedestal and fell, smashing into a hundred pieces on the wooden floor.

A tense pause followed the sound of shattering china; then Miriam leapt to her feet.

'Adrian!'

Robert glanced down at Heidi, saying cuttingly, 'I'm afraid Adrian is still very immature.'

In tears, Adrian fled from the room.

Miriam knelt by the shattered doll, distractedly picking up the pieces, and Robert laughed, turning easily to his guests.

'Never let children near champagne. They can't take it.'

* * *

By one o'clock the party had broken up. Miriam and Robert stood in the hall, saying goodnight to the last departing guest, while Ian and I sat tiredly on the settee.

We heard the front door close for the last time and then Robert saying, 'Was there any need to make such a fuss over that doll?'

Miriam's voice was shrill. 'You have the nerve to accuse me of making a scene, after your ... your ... exhibition! Why couldn't you leave the boy alone? He wasn't doing any harm. You never have had any time for him. You and your so-called work!'

'We all know what you think of my work,' Robert returned. 'You, of all people, ought to understand. You're supposed to be my wife.'

'Am I?' Miriam shouted. 'Then why don't

51

I get any consideration from you? Why do you always show me up? Look at the way you're dressed. It's just too much to believe. When will you grow up?'

We heard her footsteps pounding up the stairs and Robert's, more slowly, following.

'So it begins,' Ian said with disgust. 'That was the first skirmish in what promises to be a bloody battle.'

'Don't talk like that!' I exclaimed.

'What else can I do? There's nothing anyone can do. We have to stand by and watch those two tear each other apart.'

I turned on him, furious, my hands clenched. 'How can you say that? How can you?'

'Don't you go to pieces, too,' he said, taking my hands in his. 'Stay with me, Anne, on the outside. Don't get involved.'

I tore my hands free. 'You're too late. I'm involved already. And if I stand by anyone it will be Robert.'

'Of course,' Ian said stiffly, standing up. 'I should have had more sense ... Excuse me.'

*   *   *

Early the next morning I was roused by the tap-tap of a typewriter in the study next to my room. Slipping on slacks and a sweater, I went out on to the veranda. The sky was

52

clear, the air warm and oppressive as I walked along to the outer door of the study, where Robert sat hunched over the typewriter, slowly tapping at it with one finger, while the other hand supported his tousled head. The large ashtray beside him was full to overflowing and pieces of screwed-up paper littered the floor. As I watched, Robert jerked the paper from the machine, rolled it into a ball and hurled it across the room.

When I tapped on the door, Robert turned sharply, then came wearily to let me in. His face was grey with fatigue as he leaned on the desk looking at me.

I spread my hands to indicate the scattered paper. 'You should know that when you get to this stage you're too tired to work.'

'I've been sitting here all night and I haven't finished a single page,' he said.

'Get some sleep, Robert,' I said gently, taking his arm.

He staggered across to the couch and flopped down full length. On impulse, I bent over him, stroking his hair back, and his hand came up to grasp my wrist.

'You're good for me, Anne. Why aren't all women like you?'

'It would be a dull world if they were.'

'I'm sorry about last night. It was entirely my fault, Anne. I know it must be hell for you, but don't leave, whatever you do.'

'I won't be leaving,' I promised.

He smiled tiredly, closing his eyes, and I covered him with the travelling rug which lay across the back of the couch. Pulling the curtains partly across, I stepped quietly on to the veranda, leaving the door open to let in the fresh air.

Below me, Ian was wandering in the garden, to the accompaniment of the clatter of pots from the kitchen. He glanced up at me, unsmiling and silent, and continued his wandering.

Returning to my own room, I had gained the upper hall when I heard Miriam's voice below me as she spoke into the telephone. What I heard made me draw back and listen breathlessly.

'Yes, he's going tomorrow. It seems a good opportunity ... How? Papers? Oh, Charles, can you? Won't you be found out? ... Oh, I see. Yes, I'll meet you in town then, and collect them. I'll find a way. Can you alert the police for ... Yes, all right... You know I will. All I need is a good reason. He'll never divorce *me*. So I'll see you at about twelve. Goodbye.'

Horrified, I withdrew into my room and stood with a pounding heart, trying not to believe my own ears. Charles and Miriam were planning to steal papers from the Consulate and plant them on Robert when he went through the Wall. The arrogance of the plan seemed incredible. They couldn't hope to succeed. Or could they?

Robert was in no state to be told of his wife's plot, but I had to talk to someone. I hurried on to the veranda and down the steps, across the lawn to the beach, where Ian was sitting on a hummock of grass smoking his pipe.

'Good morning,' I called.

Ian looked round, his face set, and said distantly, 'Good morning, Mrs Holbrook.'

'Can I talk to you?' I said.

He stood up abruptly. 'Why? I thought you made yourself abundantly clear last night. Anyway, I'm just going in for breakfast.' He walked past me, stopped and turned back. 'Incidentally, I was out pretty early. I came along the veranda, I'm afraid I was a witness to the little scene in there.'

'And what do you think you witnessed?' I demanded. 'You have a nasty mind, Mr French. Robert and I are friends. We work together and we understand one another. That's all.'

Ian glowered, bending to tap out his pipe on a stone. 'It must be a very close relationship,' he growled, and left me.

Cursing myself for trying to explain to Ian something which didn't concern him, I stood staring at the ruffled water of the lake, watching the blurred reflection of grey clouds gathering in the West. The horizon was dark and the wind was rising, chopping the water. We were in for a storm, outside as well as inside the house.

In the dining-room, I found Adrian morosely picking at bacon and egg. Ian sat at the opposite end of the table, reading a book as he ate without enjoyment, and neither of them spoke as I helped myself to coffee and sat down. The silence was broken only when Miriam looked in to say she was going out.

Adrian grunted and pushed his plate away, looking across at me for the first time, with bloodshot, bleary eyes.

'She told me off something chronic,' he said.

'You deserved it,' I replied. 'I hope you've learnt your lesson.'

'Oh, don't worry,' Adrian said tartly. 'I won't say another word. I'll just pretend I'm not here, like everyone else does.'

Ian's hand slammed down on the table, making both Adrian and the cutlery jump.

'Stop being childish, Adrian!' he ordered. 'If you were a bit more pleasant to people you'd find yourself being treated like an adult instead of a spoiled brat.'

Adrian looked near to tears.

'All right,' Ian sighed. 'I've said my piece. My advice now is to apologise to your father as soon as you see him. He's not such a bad chap, you know. Now, where's that electric train set you were telling me about?'

The boy leapt to his feet, brightening. 'In the box-room. There's something wrong with it. Do you suppose you can mend it?'

The door slammed behind them and I began to clear the table. I glanced at Ian's book, but it was full of wiring diagrams and might as well have been written in Chinese.

Later in the morning I took some coffee up to the box-room on the second floor. The train set filled the whole of the floor, with Ian sitting cross-legged in the middle of the complexities of rail while Adrian straddled the miniature station, watching as his uncle worked on the transformer.

The boy grinned at me. 'Ian's just the man for this job. He'll have it going in no time.'

'We hope,' Ian added doubtfully. 'Adrian, there's a pair of pliers in a toolbox in my room. Will you fetch them?'

Carefully, Adrian picked his way to the door.

Ian glanced up at me. 'I think I owe you an apology. I rather leapt to conclusions, I'm afraid. And quite frankly I don't think either you or my brother are the type of people to...'

'We aren't,' I said swiftly. 'Strange as it may seem to outsiders, there's never been any danger of our relationship deviating

57

from the platonic. If there was, I wouldn't be here.'

'No,' Ian said slowly, his eyes on my face. 'I'm very sorry.'

'Let's forget it. I did want to talk to you about something...'

But at that moment Adrian reappeared with the pliers and once again I had to delay telling Ian of the phone conversation I had overheard.

*   *   *

Miriam did not return until after lunch and she was in a foul mood, which matched the weather. Rain had begun to deluge from a slate-grey sky and promised to continue for hours. Charles arrived before we had dinner, by which time Robert had woken, and after the meal I went to my room to finish a letter to my parents, leaving Miriam, Robert and Charles in the lounge. Adrian and Ian again went to pay homage to the train set.

It was difficult to write a letter which did not tell my parents anything of the turmoil in the house and in myself. I heard several sets of footsteps up and down the stairs, with doors opening and closing. The house was restless and outside violent thunderstorms began, lightning standing in sheets beyond the Havel and thunder cracking overhead.

I flung my pen down in disgust, with one small page of half-truths written. It was impossible to concentrate when my mind kept repeating Miriam's words of that morning. If she really was plotting against Robert, then I should tell him.

A brilliant flash of lightning made the lights flicker and I crossed swiftly to the door, flipping the switch to put my room in darkness so that I could more easily watch the storm. Carefully moving back to the window, I pulled aside the curtain as the house shook with thunder. It was pitch black outside, rain spattering heavily against the glass. As I stood there, another streak of forked lightning reared high above the lake, illuminating the water with a queer silver-blue light and leaving a red image on my retina. Blinking, I saw what appeared to be a human form pass the window towards the garage steps.

Again I thought of Miriam's conversation with Charles. If they were going to plant papers on Robert, then the study was the place to put them, probably in the briefcase he was bound to take with him to the East. Knowing Robert, he wouldn't bother to check the case before he left.

The whole thing still seemed wildly improbable and I began to doubt that I had really seen someone creep along the veranda. However, there was one way to find out.

Moving quietly, I went along the landing to the study. As I went in, the outer door flew open on a great gust of wind, sending the curtains flying and rain splashing in. The veranda door had not been properly closed. Someone *must* have been in the study illicitly.

I snapped on the light, moving to close the swinging door, and as I did so a piece of paper lifted on the wind and wrapped itself round my ankle. Forcing the door shut, I locked it and bent to pick up the paper, placing it absently on the desk before I realised that it was not one of Robert's note-sheets. I straightened it out and found myself staring at a typed copy of a secret document concerning, apparently, movements of military equipment to or from Berlin.

It was clear that Charles had carried out his plan. In the darkness he must have dropped this one paper. But where were the rest?

I began a frantic search of Robert's briefcase and all the drawers and cupboards in the room, but found nothing except the usual welter of typed and handwritten pages concerning Robert's work. I searched everywhere, until no other possible hiding place remained.

Standing with my hands braced against the desk, I thought the matter through again. There had been incriminating papers in this room—that much was confirmed by the sheet I held in my hand. Either Charles or Miriam had put them here, probably Miriam after she returned from her lunch date with Charles. It would have been easy enough for her, necessitating no skulking on the veranda, so something must have made the confederates change their minds. Perhaps Charles had thought the study too obvious a place, but with me in my room all evening they had not dared to risk being found going through the house to retrieve the documents, so one of them had gone out, up to the veranda. The question now was—what was their new plan?

And then, as I left the study, I encountered Charles on the landing. He glanced at me sharply, suspiciously, before turning into the bathroom, and when I reached my own room I shut the door and stood leaning on it, breathing hard as though I had been running. I was certain that I had guessed the truth. It had been Charles out there on the veranda. He had got wet.

That was why he had been in his shirtsleeves just now.

CHAPTER FOUR

The sky was blue again and the earth smelt sweet after the rain. I stood at my window wondering if the events of the previous night could really have happened in this world of brightness and peace. But even as the thought crossed my mind there was the sound of spasmodic gunfire from the range across the border and the double boom of a Russian jet breaking the sound barrier. The world might be bright and peaceful, but it was an uneasy peace.

If I needed any extra proof that intrigue and terror were close at hand I had only to look at the crumpled piece of paper I was holding. It told me only too clearly that I had not been dreaming.

The paper was a problem, however, for Charles would surely discover it was missing. Why had he changed his mind about leaving the documents? Had he thought of a better place to put them?

I looked around the room, searching for a hiding place for the paper. After a few minutes' thought, I picked open some stitches in the lavender sachet Mother had made for me and put the paper in among the dried flowers, resewing the edge carefully. It was my one piece of tangible evidence.

★　　★　　★

In the study after breakfast I had difficulty keeping my mind on the scrawled notes which Robert gave me to sort out. Somehow he must be warned of the plot against him.

'What's wrong, Anne?' he asked eventually. 'Are you worried about Adrian?'

'Adrian?'

'Being left on his own this afternoon? It's his own choice, you know. He likes being alone.'

'Does he? I wonder. If you don't mind my saying so, Robert, he could do with more of your company.'

Robert frowned, striking a match and holding it to the cigarette in his mouth. 'You may be right. I still think of him as a small boy.'

'But he's not. He's growing up. If you could ...' I broke off, looking away. 'I'm sorry. It's not my concern.'

'On the contrary, I'm grateful. You know how wrapped up I get. Can't see what's in front of my nose sometimes. One evening next week we'll all go down to Hühner Hugo's for a half chicken. He'll like that, won't he?'

'I'm sure he will.'

'Anything else I haven't done?' Robert asked lightly, tapping his cigarette against the cut-glass ashtray. 'For Miriam, for example? Just don't ask me to spend more time with *her*. We strike sparks every time we meet. And with Charles around she isn't starved for attention.'

'Don't you mind about Charles?'

He shrugged. 'He keeps her off my back. You've probably noticed that Miriam and I are not ... ideally suited, shall we say? We only stay on friendly terms when we're apart.'

'Yes, I know, but ...' I struggled for words. How did one tell a man that his wife was trying to destroy him?

'Well?' Robert prompted, with an amused lifting of the brows.

'There's something I must tell you,' I got out, turning hot and cold. 'Miriam and Charles ... they...'

'Yes?'

'They're trying to get rid of you,' I blurted. 'I heard them yesterday, arranging to get secret papers from the Consulate and have you arrested with them on you this afternoon, when you go through the Wall.'

'Indeed?' Robert said in a hard voice, frowning now.

'I'm afraid so. I'm sorry to have to tell you, but I thought you ought to know. And then last night, during the storm, someone

64

was on the veranda, coming from this direction. It was Charles, I'm sure. I thought he must have left the papers in here, but I searched and...'

'My dear girl!' Robert interrupted, wide-eyed. 'What an appalling story. Why didn't you tell me?'

'I would have done, but you were asleep all day. Do you have to go to East Berlin this afternoon?'

'It's not essential, but ... Where do you suppose those papers are now?'

'I don't know. I expect they thought it was too risky to leave them here. Miriam was supposed to collect them yesterday. My guess is that she put them in here and then Charles fetched them out again. It sounds pretty silly, but...'

Robert looked gravely at the cigarette in his fingers. 'No, it sounds just like them. You're probably right, Anne. But from what I know of Charles I doubt if I'm in any real danger.'

'What? But...'

'No, let me finish. You see, Charles has no serious intentions where Miriam's concerned. He may pretend he has, just to keep her sweet, but he wouldn't risk his job. I'll accept that maybe he went along with the plan, maybe even procured some documents—innocuous ones, of course— and let Miriam put them in the house. But he couldn't risk having them found. I'd guess he took them and destroyed them without telling Miriam. Come to think of it, he did go missing for a short time last night.'

'But they might try again.'

Robert laughed softly. 'So they may. But I wouldn't worry about it, Anne. Those two have no hope of harming me. They're much too naïve.'

I felt relieved. The paper I had so carefully hidden meant nothing after all. But I would keep it, just in case they did think up some other plan. It was proof of their conspiracy.

Robert was saying, 'As long as Miriam keeps out of my way I'm quite happy ... Ian, now, he's entirely different. How are you getting on with Ian, by the way?'

'Oh, I ... we ... he's all right.'

'Is that a leading question?' Robert teased. He paused, leaning both his elbows on the desk and watching the smoke curl up from his cigarette. 'In some ways, I envy Ian. He's far more practical than I am, in lots of ways. He's never been a one to come running for advice—more ready to give it. But if I'm honest he's better qualified for that sort of thing. We don't talk much, because we have no common ground. I don't think he likes me much...'

'Oh, I ...' I burst in, and Robert looked

at me, smiling slightly.

'I'm his older brother. He feels duty bound to have brotherly feeling for me, but that's all.'

'I think you're wrong,' I said.

Robert waved his cigarette in an arc. 'I can only say how it looks to me. Either way, I'm not overly bothered. My work is enough. It is family and friends to me.' Suddenly he burst out laughing, as if he had made some hilarious joke. 'God, listen to me. I'm talking like one of my characters. Stop distracting me, woman, and let's get down to work.'

Sometimes I found it difficult to tell when Robert was being serious. He was an exhilarating person to work with, but I was constantly taunted into trying to solve the unsolvable enigma that was Robert French.

★   ★   ★

The heat inside the silver-grey Mercedes was intense that afternoon, despite the cooler air rushing in through the ventilators. As we drove past the ever-burning Flame of Freedom, on Theodor Heuss Platz, the long, straight Kaiserdamm dipped away before us, bright with sunshine gleaming on the roofs of cars stretching in streams right down to the dancing fountains on Ernst Reuter Platz. Beyond, shimmering in the heat haze, the golden winged Siegessaule reached for the sky and I could just see the Brandenburg Gate in the misty distance.

As the car sped on, Robert and Ian discussed the sights of the city, but most of the conversation was lost on me. I was huddled in a corner of the back seat, silently praying that we would meet no trouble at the checkpoint and wondering if Charles had, after all, hidden the papers again, in the car perhaps.

'Chas would have been fascinated,' I heard Ian say.

'Chas who?' I asked, trying to get my mind off the problem.

Ian was about to reply when Robert made an impatient gesture. 'Charles French,' he said tersely. 'Our older brother. He was killed a few years ago.'

'He was a keen amateur historian,' Ian added. 'He'd have loved this city.'

We were passing now through the older back streets of Berlin, tall houses and shops crowding close to one another. Down one of these streets we stopped outside the wooden offices of the Allied border guard which stood in the middle of the road, and I stared up at the sign announcing that this was Checkpoint Charlie. Our passports were examined as I stared fixedly at the crossed stakes on either side of the car. They were there to hinder any storming of the Wall, which reared ahead of the car.

Eight or ten feet high and twelve feet thick, of solid concrete, the Wall here had jagged glass fixed at the top and an opening barely wide enough for the Mercedes. I was startled when I felt the car begin to slide forward.

Once inside the Eastern sector we negotiated an obstacle course which I knew was changed at irregular intervals, to prevent anyone memorising the route and racing through to the West, and freedom. At the barrier beyond, a member of the East German *Volkspolizei*—people's police—politely asked us to step into his hut to have our documents checked. To my intense relief there was no hitch.

At first we saw only the dingy back streets and the same stocky people, except that they seemed to me to be scuttling about like frightened rabbits. Then we were in the showplace called Karl Marx Allee, where a tall glass building, its sides covered in mosaic, stands at the head of a road lined by modern department stores and blocks of flats. At the other end of this impressive street are historic tower-houses, but beyond there appeared to be nothing but dilapidation. Inside the buildings there was an impression of eternal gloom as the light from naked bulbs shone out despite the bright sunlight.

At Treptow Park we left the car and walked through the gateway into the area of the Russian War Memorial, past a stone figure of a weeping woman. Geometrically placed flower beds lay before the few wide steps between huge dipped flags sculpted in red marble.

As we reached the top of these steps, several Russian soldiers, in uniform, came up from the other side and posed, laughing, for pictures beside the bronze statue at the base of the marble flags. Before us lay five rectangular lawns which covered the mass graves, and beyond them, on a small hill, the domed Mausoleum topped by a huge statue of a Russian soldier, a child in his arms and his sword resting on a crushed swastika.

A party of Americans was coming down the steps from the Mausoleum, talking loudly, with batteries of cameras slung round them, but inside the round building there was a hushed, church-like atmosphere. No one spoke as we surveyed the mosaic pictures on the walls and the crystal representation of the Soviet Order of Victory in the domed roof. Below, inside a glass case, lay the Roll of Honour.

I hurried out again, into the sunshine, being followed more slowly by the two men.

'What's the matter with you?' Robert asked.

I shuddered. 'Can we go now? This place gives me the creeps. I feel as though I'm being watched all the time.'

'Guilty conscience?' Robert teased.

I had several pages of almost illegible notes by the time Robert had finished cruising round the Soviet sector, and it was early evening before we started back to Checkpoint Charlie. Ancient, rattling trams raced beside ramshackle cars and bicycles, but the traffic was nothing like as heavy as that of West Berlin.

At the Checkpoint, the Vopos searched the car, which gave me cause for holding my breath, but eventually we were allowed back through the narrow gap and into the American sector. Only then did I wonder what Miriam would say when she knew Charles's plan had failed.

*   *   *

We were met by the pulsing beat of jazz coming from the lounge.

'Oh, God,' Robert sighed as we entered the house. 'When Miriam plays that record she's in a bad mood.'

This comment was proved correct by the abrupt appearance of his wife, her dark face twisted with anger.

'About time, too! I expect the dinner is burnt, if it isn't stone cold. Eleonore! ...

71

You can serve dinner now.'

She marched ahead of us into the dining room just as Adrian emerged from the lounge.

'Thank goodness you've come,' he whispered. 'Mother hasn't spoken to me since I got back from the zoo.'

The dinner was neither cold nor burnt, which only served to darken Miriam's mood. Our lateness may have been the cause of her irritability, but I couldn't help feeling that there was another reason—her plan to get rid of Robert had misfired.

After dinner, Miriam retired to her room, pleading a headache. Adrian found an old ball and persuaded Ian to play cricket on the lawn, while Robert and I sat at the bamboo table on the patio, discussing the notes we had made. However, it was not long before our work was interrupted by the arrival of Harry Smith.

He had come to invite us to a Guest Night at the officers' mess the following Monday and to suggest that we might like to join Selena and himself in a day on the lake. They had hired a motor-boat and were intending to have a picnic lunch on one of the islands in the lake and perhaps do some water-skiing.

Adrian viewed this plan with enthusiasm and Robert astonished me by asking to have Charles Ellistone included in the invitations.

It was finally agreed that we should take the trip the next day.

When Miriam appeared, pale and speaking in a listless voice which betokened one of her migraines, Ian announced that he was going for a walk and asked Adrian and myself to accompany him.

'Where shall we go?' Ian asked as we reached the beach.

'Let's go and have a *bockwurst*,' Adrian suggested eagerly.

'You and your *bockwurst!*' I laughed. 'Do you mind, Ian?'

'I'll go anywhere you like,' he said, looking down at me, 'as long as you'll come with me.'

For once I found no reply to that and when he took my hand I didn't argue. I was beginning to realise that Ian French was not the kind of man one could keep at arm's length.

'It looks as though we're going to have a gay old time in the next few days,' he said as we followed a high-spirited Adrian along the beach. 'But I can't understand why Robert had to include Charles in the outings. Can you?'

'No. No, I can't. But then, he doesn't suspect there's anything going on between Charles and Miriam—other than friendship.'

'There must be,' Ian said fiercely. 'Oh,

well, change the subject. Adrian's waiting for us.'

'I didn't know you had another brother,' I said.

'Oh? Yes, he was the middle one. Charles Alexander French. We always called him Chas.'

'What happened to him?'

'Who are you talking about?' Adrian demanded as we came up to him and began walking through the trees towards the waterfront.

'Your Uncle Chas,' Ian said.

'Oh, yes. I remember Uncle Chas. He was a fighter pilot, wasn't he?'

'Yes. His plane crashed—at least his base lost contact with him and later they found some bits of a fighter they thought was his. It had been burnt out, so they say. Chas's body was never recovered.'

'I'm sorry,' I said.

'We lost contact after he left school,' Ian told me. 'He was always the odd one out and after he joined the R.A.F. we hardly saw him. He visited Mother occasionally, but I was working away and Chas wasn't much for writing letters. He always got on better with Robert.'

'He used to come and see us quite often,' Adrian said. 'I remember when I was little he took me to see a cathedral—Norwich, I think it was ... Look, there's the stall.

74

Who's going to treat me to *bockwurst* tonight?'

Ian and I exchanged amused glances and Ian said fondly to his nephew, 'You utter horror.'

When we returned to the house, a light was on in the study and the lounge was empty except for Eleonore.

'*Frau* French has a bad head,' she explained. 'And *Herr* French—he is working. You wish for supper? ... *Nein?* Then I also go to bed. *Gute nacht.*'

Adrian yawned hugely. 'I'm off to bed as well. Goodnight, you two lovebirds.'

As the door closed behind the boy, Ian turned to look at me and say, 'How little he knows. Nothing could be further from the truth, could it?'

'No,' I said, though my voice lacked conviction.

'Not for you, at least.'

I turned away. 'Please, Ian, don't...'

'Don't what? Don't say "I love you"? It's what I want to say. Too soon, I know. Too damnably certain, though. It's happened. What do I have to do to get through to you?'

I closed my eyes tightly, whispering, 'I don't know.'

'Maybe if ...' His hand came on my shoulder, swung me round into his arms. He bent over me and then paused, shaking

75

his head sadly. 'No, I can't force you. I'm not made that way.'

To my surprise I felt disappointed. For a moment I had wanted him to crush me to him and ... Something of my thoughts must have shown on my face, for he bent and laid his mouth on mine for the briefest instant before moving away, reaching for his pipe.

'Ian,' I said softly, touched by his obvious dejection. 'Just give me time.'

He nodded, not looking at me. 'Goodnight, Anne.'

My fingers to my lips where his had rested, I went slowly up the stairs, wondering how long I could keep my treacherous emotions in check.

★   ★   ★

Harry and Selena Smith arrived early the following morning in the motor-boat. I saw them from my window as I was changing into a swimsuit and beach dress. Harry came loping up the path, dressed in red trunks that displayed the mat of black hairs on his chest, while Selena lounged in the boat, her body revealed by the briefest of bikinis.

By the time I went downstairs Charles had arrived and we all crammed into the boat for the short trip to the island, where we lounged around or swam as the mood

76

took us, until we ate the picnic lunch.

Afterwards the Smiths and Robert went off in the boat, while Charles and Miriam strolled away through the trees—she in the long-sleeved blouse and slacks that gave best protection from the mosquitoes. Adrian slipped into the water and swam off on an expedition of his own, leaving Ian and myself sitting on the grass together, our swimming costumes still wet from our bathe.

'Don't you want to water-ski?' he asked.

'I don't know how,' I replied.

Ian lay back, supporting his head on his hands. 'I'm afraid that's one thing I can't help you with. I've never been near a water-ski until today.'

The boat roared past, with Harry Smith hanging grimly behind, or so it appeared.

'He doesn't look any too sure of himself,' Ian said worriedly, propping himself on one elbow.

'How can you tell from here?' I asked, laughing. 'He's supposed to be an expert ... Do you want to swim again?'

'Not really. Do you?'

'No. I'm quite happy where I am.'

He rolled over on to his stomach, looking up at me. 'Coming from you, Mrs Holbrook, that is quite an admission.'

'I suppose it is.'

'Will you tell me about your husband?'

77

I looked out across the lake, where the water was gay with yachts moving in a slow, graceful dance, and I found that I wanted to tell Ian about Nigel, wanted him to understand why I felt as I did.

'He was a freelance reporter,' I said. 'When I met him he was convalescing after an accident, in the village where I lived. My father is the vicar of the parish church there ... Nigel was ... different from the boys I'd known. He was handsome and gay, full of colourful tales about his overseas assignments. I had only known him two months when we decided to get married in a hurry before he went abroad again ...' I stopped talking, remembering how it had been in those first heady days.

'And?' Ian prompted quietly.

'And ... oh, I don't know. I suppose I expected too much. I was nineteen. I'd lived in that quiet village all my life. I thought that marriage was inevitably a happy-ever-after thing, but for us it meant a flat in town, and loneliness. Nigel was always going off to some exotic place ... I didn't mind at first. I knew I had to adjust to it. But then sometimes he didn't bother to come home even when he was in London. He stayed at some hotel or other, because it was more convenient, he said. He must have realised that I was just a naïve child and not what he wanted for a wife. And

78

there were other women. When I found that out and faced him with it he told me I'd married him for better or worse and he didn't intend to change his spots just for me. I was only handy when he had nowhere better to go. I ... oh, it was my fault, too. I'd been in love with an image of my own creation. When I finally saw the real man I didn't even like him much and I made no effort to conceal my feelings. In effect, I drove him away.

'I felt utterly trapped and disillusioned. I began to hate him. And then ... he was killed, in Biafra, at the start of the Nigerian Civil War. I felt responsible for that for a long time, as if I'd willed him to die. I went home, but it wasn't the same, so I took this job with Robert just to get away from everything. And I resolved never to get in such a mess again. Love can't be trusted.'

'But you didn't love him,' Ian argued. 'You said so yourself. You were too young to know you were only in love with love. It wouldn't happen again. You'd make sure of that. And I ... I'd give you time to be sure.' He laid his hand on my arm, adding quietly, 'Trust me, Anne. I'll never hurt you.'

As I looked down into his blue eyes and saw the warmth and sincerity in them, I knew that it was the truth—if I could let myself believe in Ian, and in myself, there was hope, even now, of lasting happiness.

79

We sat close together, his arm loosely round my shoulders, smoking cigarettes in companionable silence and watching the motor-boat roar around the island with Robert in tow and then Selena, but Ian was alarmed when it came into view with both Harry Smith and Robert skimming along behind. Selena was at the helm and now Charles was also in the boat.

'What are they fooling about at?' Ian said angrily, leaping to his feet as the two skiers came close together and moved apart again.

I stood beside him, suddenly cold with fear as I saw Charles lean over the stern of the boat and fiddle with the tow-rope.

Selena began to throw the boat from side to side, so that the skiers tossed and bumped over its wake in a swinging zig-zag movement, and I heard Robert's laugh come clearly over the water. Then, so swiftly that it had happened before anyone could avoid it, the waves from the boat met the wash of a passing barge. The two men wobbled towards each other. And collided.

Ian was running immediately, diving into the lake towards the place where thrashing water marked the situation of the two men. I went after him, but the boat had turned and come back by the time I reached the spot. Harry Smith was spluttering and gasping, dog-paddling to keep himself afloat, but Robert lay limp in Ian's arms, with blood trickling from a deep cut at his temple.

Between them, the men lifted the unconscious Robert into the boat and covered him with a blanket. Then Ian turned on Smith and let loose his rage.

'What the hell were you playing at? Robert's a novice at this game.'

Smith went pale and his wife said in a small voice, 'It was Robert's idea. He wanted more speed, he said. He told me to start weaving the boat when they were going well. I . . .'

'You didn't have to do it!' Ian thundered.

'He knew what he was doing,' Smith said harshly. 'He must have banged his head on the ski—they're lethal when they're flying about. It could have happened to me just as easily.'

Ian took a deep breath and said more calmly, 'Yes, I suppose it could.' He glanced back at Selena. 'What are you standing there for? Get this boat going.'

CHAPTER FIVE

Since Miriam was too shaken to go to the hospital it was Ian who went in the ambulance with Robert, while the Smiths took the rest of us back to the house. They

81

resisted Miriam's invitation to stay and after saying words of commiseration they went away in the hired boat.

Miriam and Charles settled together in the lounge, both of them pale and silent, while Adrian and I climbed the stairs to change out of our wet costumes.

'Are you going to have a bath?' I asked as we reached the landing.

Adrian shrugged. 'I suppose so ... Mrs Holbrook, will he be all right?'

'I think so. Don't worry, Adrian.'

'It'll be awful if he dies,' the boy said disconsolately.

'Come and sit down a minute,' I suggested, opening the door of my room. He followed me in and sat on the wooden chair by the door, his head hanging.

'Adrian ... He won't die. He just bumped his head.'

'A boy at school got kicked in the head playing football,' he said dully. 'He had concussion, and he died.'

'Now stop that!' I admonished. 'A lot of people get concussed, but most of them recover. I'm sure your father will be all right.'

Adrian suddenly flung his arms around me, burying his face against me and sobbing. Feeling totally inadequate, I stroked his hair, murmuring words of comfort.

At last he laid his hot cheek against me and dashed away his tears.

'I don't hate him,' he said brokenly. 'I wish I could tell him.'

'Then why don't you? He's human as well, you know. He needs to know you love him.'

He sat up and managed a smile. 'I'm carrying on like a girl.'

'Of course you aren't. It isn't unmanly to show emotion. Now go and have your bath. Before you know it, Ian will be back and he'll tell us exactly what's wrong with your father. Okay?'

'Okay.'

The four of us sat reading in the lounge, amid an atmosphere of impatient waiting. Charles persistently rattled his paper and fidgeted, a tiny gold cigarette holder clenched between his teeth. Miriam was chain-smoking, too, and staring unseeingly at an open magazine, while Adrian lay full length on the floor with his head in a James Bond novel.

I glanced down at the boy, wondering if he could feel the uneasiness in the other two. Were they hoping that Robert would die?

The cigarette holder made small clicking noises as Charles rolled it round his mouth. Just what, I wondered, had he been doing to the ropes on the boat? Had it all been planned? Was the 'accident' another deliberate attempt to do away with Robert?

The cuckoo clock on the wall behind me whirred and the little wooden bird came out nine times. Miriam eased herself out of the chair and walked across to the clock, pulling the dangling chains to wind it up. She was consulting her watch when the telephone in the hall rang and she went quickly to answer it.

When she returned a few moments later her face was pale.

'It was Ian,' she announced. 'Robert has not recovered consciousness yet. Ian is going to stay until he does.'

Charles cleared his throat. 'Bad job, old girl.'

There was a loud snap as Adrian closed his book and leapt to his feet. 'I'll go to bed and read. Let me know if there's any more news.'

Making the excuse of an unfinished letter to my parents, I left Charles and Miriam alone.

As I went up the stairs I had an overwhelming desire to go into the study, where I moved around to tidy the papers strewn about the desks, hoping that soon Robert would be in this room again, despite the efforts of his wife and her lover.

I was drawing the curtains when the door opened and to my astonishment Charles came in. My heart thumping with alarm, I faced him across Robert's desk.

'What do you want?'

Charles's eyes widened innocently. 'My dear Mrs Holbrook, why so touchy?'

'Leave me alone.'

'You know,' he said pleasantly, stroking his thin moustache with a plump forefinger, 'you're an attractive piece. Never noticed until I saw you in that bathing suit. Oversight on my part, what? Tired of scrawny, tough old birds, I am. Fancy something a shade plumper—more tender.' He turned to lock the door with an air of self-confidence.

I stared at him in horror, the scene on the lake flashing across my mind. 'You're tired of Miriam?' I gasped. 'And yet you tried to get rid of Robert?'

Charles blinked. 'I did?'

'You were fiddling with the ropes. I saw you.'

He laughed, waving one hand in the air. 'Selena … she asked me to make sure they were secure. Before she started swinging the boat, don't y'know. Fertile imagination you have.'

'And you're a facile liar!' I snapped.

'Thank you.' He executed a mocking bow and took a step towards me.

'Stay away from me,' I warned.

'Oh, come, my dear. A widow, are you

not? No unspoiled schoolgirl. I'll show you a thing or two. Mutual benefit, eh? I've more experience than young French.'

At the mention of Ian I lost my head. I made a dash for the veranda door, but Charles was surprisingly quick. He threw me on to the floor and himself on top of me, his hands grasping at my blouse. With a strength born of terror I rolled over, brought my foot up and kicked out at him. Charles fell backwards but was up as soon as I and came between me and the door.

'Spirited, aren't you?' he got out. 'Now come, Anne, don't fight me. I won't hurt you.'

Trembling with fear and rage I stood docilely until he came very near to me, and then I brought my knee up sharply. He bent double, moaning with pain.

After fighting to unlock the door, I fled to my room, flinging the door open. But there was to be no respite yet. Miriam was sitting on my bed, her green eyes sparking fire in the light from the landing.

'I saw him follow you and guessed what was coming,' she said flatly. 'He gets like that sometimes, but he always comes back to me. He doesn't realise he's getting old and fat and young girls don't find him attractive any more.'

I stared dazedly at her, my breath coming swiftly and painfully. 'He comes back?' I said incredulously. 'And you let him? I thought you had more pride.'

Miriam laughed shortly. 'Pride doesn't keep you warm in bed. Look at me—I have to take what I can get. And I'm hanging on to Charles. He'll leave you alone after this. You've damaged his ego. He'll turn to me for consolation.'

'But you have Robert.'

'No one has Robert, except Robert. There's nothing left between us—not a shred.'

'I don't believe you,' I gasped. 'You can't be seeing clearly. Charles is no good to anyone.'

Miriam stood up, her fingers curled into claws. 'Charles is mine. You stand there, confident in your youth, while I ... I have never been physically attractive. What do you know of my feelings? How can I describe the years of misery? But it has nothing to do with you. When you leave, Charles will be all mine.'

I faced her angrily, my hands clenched. 'You must be mad. Do you seriously think I would leave Robert to your mercy?'

Her eyes narrowed. She said furiously, 'You will have to leave when Robert is dead!'

For the space of a second I stood completely still, paralysed by her words; then I turned and ran down the stairs and out of the house, knowing only that I must get away from the choking atmosphere of the building. I ran blindly through the darkness until I could run no more. Driven by a desire to avoid thinking, I continued to wander, picking my way through deep shadows under the lakeside trees. But the thoughts stayed with me. 'When Robert is dead'—Miriam's words pounded at my brain with every step I took.

At last, realising that I was wandering without purpose or direction, I stopped, breathing in great gasping sobs. I was on the rough road from the beach to the waterfront at Kladow—the road where, only last night, I had walked so happily with Ian and Adrian. Ian—surely he would be home by now? I longed for the reassurance of his solid presence.

Turning back towards the house, I began to walk slowly along the beach. The moon was bright and, by its light, I glanced at my watch. It was almost midnight.

Then I paused abruptly, frozen into stillness by the sight of a shadow that stumbled from the trees ahead of me—a tall, thin shadow, staggering. Everything but an unnamed dread was banished from my mind. The shadow fell to one knee, bending low over the ground as if in pain, and pushed itself erect with a great effort, taking slow, painful steps into the moonlight. The man stopped when he saw me and slowly held out his hands in supplication.

His words only just reached my ears, spoken in an anguished whisper—'*Helfen mir! Bitte, helfen mir!*'

The cry for help was so genuine that I felt a surge of pity for the thin, bent figure. He lifted his face and I saw the gash across his cheek, turned black by the moonlight.

'*Helfen mir!*' he said again, and something else which I didn't understand.

I stepped forward, forgetting every word of German I knew. 'I'm sorry, I...'

A ghost of a smile flitted across his gaunt face, leaving a glimmer of hope in the shadows. 'Thank God! You're English ... I've ... just escaped ... from the East ...' He groaned and fell to one knee.

The East! In alarm, I glanced out across the dark, quiet lake. 'We must get you to a hospital. I'll go and phone.'

'No!' he said desperately, clutching at my wrist. 'No, please. I'm not badly hurt. Just tired and ... wet.'

In the midst of my panic-stricken thoughts I remembered the red-faced Bracke, who was surely the ideal person to turn to in these circumstances.

I bent to take the man's arm. His clothes were wringing wet, clammy with cold, and his shoes were dangling round his neck.

'There's a police chief lives near here.

He'll help you.'

He withdrew from me, shivering. 'No! No one must know. Don't you understand? I have to get out of Berlin. It means my life.'

'But I can't do anything for you,' I protested. 'We must go to the authorities.'

'No. If you can't help I'll ... find some way out myself.'

He was shaking with cold now and I felt responsible for him. How could I leave him alone in this state? As he sank again to the ground, I pressed my hands to my head, too overwrought to think clearly. Perhaps the man could stay overnight in the house. A few hours would surely do no harm and tomorrow ... tomorrow I would feel more able to cope. He was obviously on the point of collapsing. My tired mind refused to think any further.

'All right,' I said wearily. 'Here, take my arm. I'll get you to the house where I live.'

'You mustn't tell anyone else.'

'No. No, I won't. Let me help you.'

At last he was on his feet and leaning heavily on me. His breathing was laboured and I felt the cold wetness of his clothes with every step he took. But he was in my charge now. My instinct bade me protect him.

From the bottom of the lawn I could see that lights were still on in the lounge. At sight of them my reasoning began to function, ringing alarm bells. Suppose the man were a criminal? He might be anything... But behind the rushing fears a small voice was reminding me of the gash on his face, his obvious desperation. It was all too real to be untrue.

I had some hazy idea of letting the man stay in my room for the night, but as I looked at the house the moonglow fell on the study door like a guiding beacon. The study was the ideal place for the man. With Robert in hospital, I was the only one who had a key to it. I could lock the man in—to protect him and to protect the other occupants of the house, in case he was not telling the truth.

'You'll have to go up to the veranda,' I whispered. 'The second door along. Wait there and I'll come and open it for you as soon as I can.'

He went slowly up the steps by the garage, on hands and feet like an animal. Halfway up he stumbled and turned to look at me with wide, hunted eyes. In the silence my heartbeats seemed to thunder, but there was no sound from the lighted lounge. I motioned the man on and stood watching until he was safely outside the study door, where he sat down to wait.

Praying that Charles would not be there, I stepped on to the patio and opened the french doors.

Miriam was alone in the room, having been waiting for me to come in before she went to bed. There was no more news from the hospital, she informed me distantly, her cold eyes surveying the patches of damp and traces of mud on my clothes.

'I fell over,' I said. 'Slipped and fell at the edge of the lake.'

Miriam sniffed disdainfully and turned away. 'We may as well retire. Ian may not be back for hours.'

In my room, I leaned against the door, listening until Miriam had come upstairs and gone to her own room; then I forced myself into action again. Carrying a couple of blankets, I crept out on to the dark landing and along to the study door, silently praying that Robert would forgive me for making use of his study in this manner. Having closed and locked the door, I dropped the blankets on the couch and switched on the reading lamp on Robert's desk.

In the shaft of light falling through the half-drawn curtains I could see the refugee still sitting on the veranda, his knees drawn up and his head hanging between them. I thought he was asleep, but as I opened the door he glanced up sharply, looking relieved, and crawled into the study.

His eyes were pale with tiredness in his rugged face as he picked himself up painfully and stared at me.

'Get those wet things off,' I hissed. 'Put one of those blankets round you. I'll get some soap and water. Quickly, before you catch a chill.'

The man began stripping off his soaking sweater and I noted that already there was a ring of water drops at his feet. Feeling like an intruder myself, I crept across the landing and fetched a bowl of water, some soap and a towel from the bathroom.

When I returned to the study, the man was huddled in a blanket on the couch, his head bent in misery. His clothes lay in a bedraggled heap and they smelt foul with lake water as I switched on the radiator and draped sweater, trousers and socks over it.

'Are these all the clothes you have?' I asked.

He nodded glumly.

'Shall I wash that cut on your face? How did it happen?'

'I crossed the border,' he said flatly. 'You can imagine the rest—barbed wire, minefields, and that stinking lake.'

'You're safe now,' I said, feeling genuinely sorry for the wretched man.

He looked up, his eyes wide and anxious. 'I'm not! I must get out of Berlin. Will anyone find me here?'

'No, you're safe for a while. The man who owns this house is in hospital. Only he and I ever use this study—I'm his secretary. I'll keep the door locked.'

'Can you get me out of Berlin?'

'Me?' I breathed incredulously. 'But I ... oh, really...'

'Please!' He held out his hand. 'Who else can I ask? I'm sorry that you were the one to find me, but you did. And no one else must know. Please help me. And please, please don't tell anyone else. Not anyone.'

Not even Ian? I thought wildly. But I had to tell Ian. I could do nothing alone. It was impossible.

'Promise me!' the refugee said urgently. 'You have no idea what would happen if ... Please help me.'

'I don't know,' I sighed, feeling unutterably weary. 'Let me think about it.' I studied his upturned face, seeing that he was younger than I had at first thought. The blanket had slipped from his shoulder, revealing pale skin that was red with numerous scratches.

He gazed back at me. 'I'm very grateful, Miss...'

'Anne,' I said. 'What's your name?'

'Anything you like. Some people call me Al.'

'Short for Alan?'

He shrugged. 'It's as good a name as any.'

I fetched him some food from the kitchen

and finally locked him in before going to bed. Despite my worry over Robert I fell asleep almost at once.

*　　*　　*

By morning I was still of the opinion that I should tell Ian about the man I had found on the beach, but as it happened he gave me no chance. I was still in bed when he came to say goodbye before leaving for work.

'I mustn't stay long,' he said as he perched on the bed. 'I don't want to be late on my first morning.'

'How's Robert?' I asked. 'What time did you get home?'

'About two a.m. Robert's going to be all right, but they're keeping him in for a few days. Concussion. But what I want to know is—what happened last night? Miriam said there was a scene of some kind.'

'It was Charles. He cornered me in the study and tried to ...'

'I'll kill him!' Ian exclaimed, clasping my hands convulsively.

'He didn't hurt me,' I said hurriedly. 'I think I hurt him—I hope I did. But then ... Miriam was waiting for me. She knew what was going on, Ian, but she just sat and waited. She said Charles always goes back to her after he's ... She said Robert was going to die.'

'Well, he isn't. She must be out of her mind. Stay away from her, Anne. I really must go now.'

'But there was something else I wanted to...'

Ian glanced at his watch. 'Later, love. I'll see you tonight. I'll be thinking about you.' He bent forward and kissed me perfunctorily before heading for the door.

* * *

When I was dressed, I slipped down to the kitchen and prepared myself a breakfast tray, telling Eleonore that I intended to get on with some work while I ate and that I would return the tray when I had finished. I carried it back to the study, locking the door after me as the refugee emerged from his hiding place behind the couch. His clothes were crumpled and dirty, but at least they were dry.

'Can you help me any more?' he asked through mouthfuls of food. 'I have no right to ask, but...'

'No, you haven't. One thing I want to know—why must you leave the city? Surely you're safe now you've reached this sector?'

'No. You see, I ... lived here, before. I got involved with a girl who ... well, to put it bluntly, she was an agent. By the time I found out, I was wanted for questioning

96

myself—for associating with her; so I defected. She was going to the East, you see. It seemed the easiest way out. But once we got there she dropped me like a hot brick. She was just using me. I was stuck in a camp near Luckenwalde, my movements restricted. I'd been there for nearly four years when I escaped, but you see ...' He glanced around the room and shivered. 'They might still want me—the authorities here. I swear I haven't done anything, but I just couldn't stand to be taken in and questioned and ... I couldn't take any more, Anne. I have to get to West Germany. If I can get through the corridor...'

'Without a passport?'

The hope which had lit his face died suddenly. 'That's the problem, isn't it? Someone would have to smuggle me. Have you got a car?'

'I have, but ...' I bit my lip, thinking hard and studying him. He was very tall and big-boned although he was so thin. He was about Robert's height and he had a similar stoop and shape of jaw, though his mouth was different.

Going to Robert's desk, I opened the small top drawer and took out his passport. Faint hope though it was, it was all I had. The refugee watched me intently as I opened the passport.

In the photograph, Robert looked grim. He might well have been posing for a police photographer. His hair was close-cropped, as was the refugee's, and his jaw was set, making hollows in his cheeks. The photograph was some years old and did bear some resemblance to the man who stood facing me.

The written description—Colour of hair, fair. Eyes, blue. Height, 6ft 1½ins—might well have meant Alan.

I held out the passport and he took it from me slowly, hopefully, staring down at the photograph for a long time without speaking.

'Well?' I prompted. 'What do you think? If you don't want to risk it...'

Without looking up, he said, 'Oh, yes, yes ... it's better than I could have hoped for.'

I felt uncomfortable, as if I were betraying Robert in some way. 'I shall have to drive you through the corridor so that I can bring the passport back. With Robert in hospital it should be all right. Later, I shall probably have to tell him, but I think he would understand.' I reached out and took the passport from him. 'I'll keep it for you.'

'You don't trust me?' he said, amused.

'Why should I? I don't really know why I'm helping you. It could mean a lot of trouble.'

He leaned across the desk, pleading with

me. 'I swear to you I have done nothing wrong. I wouldn't have you take this risk if I weren't desperate. Believe me, Anne.'

Oddly enough, I did believe him. I could imagine Ian's reaction if he knew of this, but deep inside me I was convinced that this man, this refugee, was trustworthy.

'I suppose I must believe you,' I said levelly. 'All right, we'll start out early tomorrow.'

'Tomorrow?'

'I can't go today,' I said irritably. 'It would look odd if I dashed off so quickly. Besides, I have to ask my employer for permission. He won't mind, I'm sure, but it's best to ask. When everyone is asleep tonight I'll take you to my car. You'll have to sleep in it, but we'll start as early as possible in the morning. Meantime, I'll bring you what food I can, though it may not be much.'

Alan smiled at me, a singularly sweet smile. 'I don't know how to thank you, Anne.'

So it was done and I was committed to helping the refugee. I might have told Ian before, but now it was too late. I had given my word. Besides which, I knew that Ian would think I was crazy. He wouldn't understand why I trusted Alan. He would want to go straight to the authorities—that was the kind of man he was—and that would mean more trouble for a man who had already suffered enough.

There was another thing, too—I might be courting trouble for myself and I had no right to involve Ian. If all went well, he need never know that anything had happened.

With a great deal of regret and soul-searching, I put out of my mind all thoughts of telling anyone else about the refugee.

★   ★   ★

I had just left the study when Adrian came pounding down the upper flight of stairs, wearing his bathing trunks and carrying his flippers.

'I thought we might go for a swim,' he said. 'Are you coming?'

'I might join you later.'

'I'll be on the beach. By the way, I forgot to tell you ... Guess what I saw yesterday.'

'I have no idea,' I said, in no mood for guessing games.

Adrian looked around, then bent to whisper in my ear. '*Oberkommissar* Bracke was in a motor-boat on the lake. He was watching us. With binoculars.'

A sigh escaped me. 'Oh, come off it, Adrian. Surely you...'

'I surfaced right behind him,' Adrian interrupted. 'It was just after lunch, but that motor-boat had been around all day. He was definitely watching us.'

'Why on earth would *Oberkommissar*...'

'Can't you guess?' His face was alight with excitement. 'You know what his job is—chasing spies.'

'So?' I said wearily.

'So ... I'll tell you something else. I ...' He stopped and looked round as his mother came down the stairs and along the landing towards us.

'Good morning, Anne,' she greeted pleasantly. 'Adrian, run along, darling. I want to speak to Mrs Holbrook.'

'Okay,' Adrian said and, to me, 'See you later. Don't forget.'

Miriam was clearly undecided as to what she was going to say and stood looking down at her slippered feet on the carpet.

'Anne, I ... that is ... Charles asked me ... to apologise to you. He was terribly upset about the whole thing and, of course, wanted to assure you it would not occur again. And I feel I should apologise also, for what I said. I would never do anything to hurt Robert, but you can't blame me for wishing there was some way of ...' She stopped talking as she looked up and saw the contempt on my face.

'I'm sorry,' I said, 'but I do blame you. You must be mad to want to swap Robert for Charles.'

Her dark face contorted into a sneer. 'I should have known better than to appeal to you. What do you know of the real Robert? I'm well aware that you are exceptionally fond of him, but of course he is always pleasant to you.' She tossed her head, switching swiftly to her mistress-of-the-household voice. 'Charles is coming for the day. I don't need to tell you to stay out of the way. You can fetch my green dress from the cleaner's. And you can keep Adrian amused.' She turned, effectively dismissing me, and ran lightly down the stairs.

Taking the breakfast tray down to the kitchen, I made a point of thanking Eleonore for the delicious meal, then I returned to the hall, just as the doorbell rang. It was the postman, with a registered letter from Robert's publishers.

I was about to close the door when a movement across the road caught my eye—Charles was getting out of his car and crossing the track to where a woman stood beneath the trees. I was surprised to recognise *Frau* Decker, Heidi's mother. Charles exchanged a few words with her and then gave her something before shaking her hand in farewell. What was all that about? I wondered as I closed the door and made my way out into the garden.

I hardly knew what I was doing any more. Everyone I knew seemed to have reason to cheat and lie and now I was becoming one of them. I felt like a fly, caught in a vast cobweb where every struggle to escape only entangled me more. The one person who might have helped—Ian—was being shut off by the wall of lies which I myself was building. I had not told him about the paper that was still hidden in my room, or about the refugee. I couldn't tell him, fearing his logical arguments against which I had only female intuition. Perhaps I was wrong, but only time would tell.

Adrian was swimming but came ashore when he saw me, dragging his flippered feet through the shallows.

'Aren't you coming in?'

'Not now. I have things to do. What were you going to tell me?'

His expression immediately became conspiratorial and he lowered his voice. 'Yesterday, before we went out, I heard a phone conversation—well, some of it. Mrs Holbrook, there's a spy in the house!'

I caught my breath sharply, staring at him. 'What are you saying, Adrian?'

'And also,' the boy went on, ignoring me, 'I know who it is. But I'm not saying.'

'Now listen,' I said, alarmed. 'If you're serious, we must talk to the *Oberkommissar*.'

'He wouldn't believe me without evidence, would he? No. But I'm doing a bit of detective work, and when I have something ... then I'll go to Bracke.'

'At least tell me what you think you heard.'

'It was about papers and money. I'm not saying any more just now. But you wait and one of these days there'll be an awful stink. I'll show them!'

I was exasperated now. 'You're imagining things!' I snapped. 'You can't accuse someone of spying just because they talked about papers and money. It could have been anything. If you go snooping around, you'll get yourself into trouble.'

'Then why was Bracke watching us?'

'He was out for the day, I expect, as we were. Bird-watching or something.'

'Huh!' Adrian snorted disgustedly. 'I might have known you wouldn't believe me.'

'Of course I don't believe a trumped-up story like that! It's too many James Bond novels, that's your trouble—and all the loose talk that went on at the party. No wonder you're imagining things.'

He scowled at me and somehow I felt better, even managing to laugh at his expression. 'Oh, never mind, Adrian. It's something else to tell the boys at school. Come on, let's see if Eleonore has some coffee on. She might even have some of those chocolate biscuits you're so fond of.'

As we went down the path, Adrian caught

my arm, pointing to where the gardener, Wilhelm, was digging behind a bush.

'Do you suppose he heard?' the boy asked.

'Heard what? Your flights of fancy? Look, Adrian, do stop playing cops and robbers. Wilhelm doesn't speak any English, anyway.'

The gardener stood up, nodding towards us. '*Guten Tag.*'

'*Guten Tag,*' I replied. 'You look busy.'

Wilhelm frowned. '*Bitte?*'

'Busy ... working.'

He shrugged. '*Nicht verstehen.*'

'*Sie tun haben,*' Adrian put in.

'*Jah, jah,*' Wilhelm agreed, wiping his brow expressively before bending over his spade again.

'I didn't know you spoke German,' I remarked to Adrian.

He grinned smugly. 'Well, I do—a bit. I've been taking it at school. It's been a help these last few days.'

'How?'

He smiled at me witheringly. 'Oh, Mrs Holbrook, you wouldn't believe me if I told you.'

I turned away irritably, not wanting to encourage him in his schoolboy fantasies. But if he had overheard a telephone conversation, and especially if it had been in German—then without a doubt he had misunderstood.

★   ★   ★

I managed to take some milk and biscuits to the refugee after lunch, prior to heading for town with a morose Adrian. We both knew only too well that Miriam wanted us out of the way while she entertained Charles. There was nothing I could do to help Adrian but chatter on about nothing in an effort to take his mind off what was going on at the house, but my own thoughts kept wandering—the refugee; the trip through the Corridor; Miriam and Charles; Robert; and Ian, of course, though for the moment my love life was the least of my worries.

'What are you thinking about?' Adrian broke in. 'You look scared. Are you all right?'

'Fine. I'm fine. It's this traffic. I have to concentrate hard.'

'If I were Ian,' the boy said, 'I'd marry you. You don't seem right, somehow, on your own. It's all right for a man, but a woman needs someone to take care of her.'

'Is that so, grandfather?' I teased. 'Haven't you heard of Women's Lib?'

'Oh, that! That's nonsense. You seem lonely. Mother doesn't like you. Dad only talks to you about work. You have no one of your own. But I bet you could have Ian.

106

And me. I'll be your best friend. Can I?'

I was touched by his appeal, for Adrian was the lonely one. Feeling rejected by his parents, he turned to me, seeing a kindred spirit.

I pulled into a parking space on the Ku'damm and turned to smile at him. His eyes, unguarded for once, were mutely appealing.

'You and I,' I said, 'are already best friends. And we always shall be, whatever happens.'

This was a remark that I was to remember, with bitterness.

⋆   ⋆   ⋆

Adrian was still contentedly watching the traffic when I emerged from a chemist's shop after buying toilet requisites for the refugee. Since he had only his disreputable clothes I had thought it wise to buy him a razor and toothbrush. I intended to get him a new sweater, too. Putting the parcel discreetly in the back of the car, I turned to Adrian.

'Where's the cleaner's?' he asked.

'Not far from here, but I want to get something else first.'

'What?' he demanded.

'A sweater ... for my brother's birthday.'

'I didn't know you had a brother.'

'Which just goes to show you don't know everything,' I replied crisply, annoyed mostly by the necessity of another lie.

Adrian pulled a face at me as I walked across his path and into a department store. It occurred to me that I was doing an awful lot for the refugee, but then, he had asked for nothing but an escape route. It was my own idea to buy him these things, in order to make him look a little more respectable.

Choosing a dark blue sweater such as Robert might have worn, I carried it with me as we went to collect Miriam's dress from the dry cleaner's.

After having a cup of tea at the Café Kranzler—where we met Heidi and her bodyguard, the girl telling us she was soon going to work in East Berlin—Adrian and I walked slowly back along the Ku'damm, looking into the wide shop windows. The pavements were crowded with shoppers and people returning home after the day's work and the traffic was growing thicker as the end of the afternoon approached.

Adrian had paused at the edge of a crowd watching an intricate train set-up in one of the windows, and was trying to push his way to the front when I caught his arm.

'Come on, Adrian. It's getting late. You can have a look at that some other time.'

He came unwillingly, his face set in a sullen frown, but he kept pace with me as I hurried to a pedestrian crossing. As we reached the kerb, the light opposite turned red and the traffic began to move again, blocking our way. A jostling crowd built up behind us.

Then suddenly, without warning, the boy plunged forward at a stumbling run—right into the path of a yellow double-decker.

CHAPTER SIX

A woman in the crowd shrieked and I heard myself scream Adrian's name as he teetered in front of the bus. He regained his balance and ran on across the road, to be blocked from sight by the moving traffic. The bus driver, braking, shouted angrily and waved his fist, while behind me the crowd were arguing and gesticulating, some of them pointing along the pavement. A woman at my side caught my arm and burst into a torrent of words.

Bewildered, I shook my head. But I had gathered that some of the crowd did not think Adrian had stepped into the road of his own volition.

When the lights changed, I ran across the wide road to where a pale and shaking Adrian was leaning against a shop window. I took his arm and made him walk with me, away from the curious people.

'What on earth were you thinking about?' I asked sharply.

Adrian gulped and wiped his forehead with a grubby handkerchief. 'Someone pushed me. I thought I'd had it. I've never been so scared.'

'But who ...?' I began.

The boy shook his head jerkily. 'I didn't see. One minute I was standing on the kerb—the next I was flying under a bus. I can still feel the imprint of two hands on my back.'

'Are you sure? I mean, it wasn't accidental, was it?'

'Of course it wasn't. I was braced against the crowd. Someone gave me a hefty shove.'

I hustled him into the car, where we had more privacy, and asked him why he should think anyone would want to push him.

Adrian took a deep breath and brushed his hair back. 'It must be because of what I heard. You know—I told you this morning.'

'You can't be serious,' I frowned.

'Why not? Now I know for sure that there's something going on.'

'Adrian,' I insisted. 'You must tell me what you heard.'

'No, not yet. And you must promise not to tell anyone else. It's our secret, for now. If I do find anything out, I'll come straight to you and tell you.'

'Is that a promise?'

'Yes, I swear it. But I'm still not certain I'm right. You see, if we talk to anyone else and then I'm wrong ... they'll laugh at me. Let's find out for sure before we do anything.'

Reluctantly, I nodded, still privately thinking he was making the whole thing up. It would be like him if he had conceived this whole incident to add weight to the story. Perhaps someone had leaned a little hard on him and given him the idea. It couldn't possibly be true.

★   ★   ★

Charles was still at the house when we returned, but by that time Ian was back from work and we had tea almost immediately.

'I've given Eleonore the evening off,' Miriam said as she poured tea. 'Adrian ... pass this cup to Ian. I hope you'll be all right on your own.'

Adrian looked surprised. 'Who? Me? Oh, I can look after myself.'

'Pity you can't come,' Charles said. 'Too young. I suppose.'

'Yes,' Miriam agreed. 'No one under eighteen is allowed in the officers' mess.'

'Anyway, I don't want to go,' Adrian said through a mouthful of bread and butter.

111

'What fun is there in boozing and dancing?'

Ian grinned at him. 'You'll find out in a few years' time.'

'Are you going to see Robert?' Miriam enquired.

'I am.' A hard glint appeared in Ian's eyes. 'Are you coming?'

Miriam concentrated on spreading a roll with butter, saying, 'I really haven't the time, as we're going out. I expect Anne will go with you.'

'Of course I will,' I said. 'We might take Adrian along, if he wants to go.'

'Not tonight,' Adrian said. 'Ian brought me a new engine. I want to try it out. I can always go some other time.'

★　　★　　★

Since Eleonore was absent, it was left to me to clear the table, which gave me an opportunity to sneak a piece of cheese and a couple of rolls up to the study. The refugee was still sleeping soundly, so I left the food on Robert's desk along with the two parcels I had brought for him, writing an explanatory note.

The sleeping man looked extraordinarily childlike and helpless now, despite the aggressive masculinity of him. He was curled up on his side, one hand under his head, and I found myself staring down at him, troubled by my feelings. I knew nothing about him, yet I trusted him and was prepared to take a great risk for his sake. Why was that?

★   ★   ★

When I had changed into my prettiest summer dress, I found Ian waiting for me in the hall. He smiled at me and took my hand, telling me that I looked lovely. For some unknown reason I wanted to cling to him and ask him to save me—though from what I had no idea. It was a crazy impulse that was gone as soon as we left the house.

'Do you mind if I drive?' he asked. 'I've got to get used to driving on the right. It was hair-raising in town today.'

'It always is,' I said feelingly as I slid into the Kharmann Ghia.

After a little fumbling and swearing, unused to the left-hand drive, he managed to back the car out of the drive, and when we were safely on the mud road he grinned at me.

'So far so good. Just yell if I'm doing something wrong. I don't want to ruin your car.'

'I'll keep my eye on you,' I said teasingly, as the car moved away. 'I missed you today.'

Ian raised his eyebrows. 'Did you? That's

113

nice to know. I missed you, too. Funny how I've got used to having you around.'

'The attraction of proximity,' I said.

Ian glanced at me sharply. 'That isn't all it is and you know it.'

'Isn't it?' I looked away, out of the window, feeling uncomfortable about what I had to do. 'How can we be sure of that? I'm confused, Ian. Don't you think it would be a good idea if I were to go away for a few days? I might as well take this opportunity. I can't do much work while Robert's in hospital, and with things as they are between Miriam and me...'

'I suppose it wouldn't do any harm,' Ian said slowly. 'I don't want you to go, but you could do with a break. Anyway, I'm in no position to stop you. You're a free agent.'

Silently I agreed with him. I *was* free—free to choose whether I wanted a new romance and free to decide for myself what was best for a tormented man who was trusting in me. I hated to deceive Ian, but it seemed the best way for everyone.

'Talking of Miriam,' Ian said after a few moments' silence, 'how was she today?'

'She apologised for the scene—rather half-heartedly. Charles was very polite and distant. He's been there all day.'

'So I gathered,' Ian said grimly. 'I could cheerfully throttle Miriam. As soon as Robert's out of the way, she openly invites

114

her lover—getting rid of you and Adrian as well, the bitch!'

'Yes,' I said quietly. 'Ian, is Robert really going to be all right?'

'Yes, but they're keeping him in for a few days. It's normal practice, apparently, for cases of concussion. I had a word with him before I left ... Anne, what did you think of that accident?'

I turned to look at him, startled. 'Why?'

'I told Robert he was lucky, that it could have been worse. I was trying to cheer him up, but ... he said, "It should have been worse". They'd given him an injection to make him sleep and at that point I was firmly asked to leave.'

'Perhaps he noticed that Charles ... Did you see what he was doing on the boat?'

'I saw, yes. That man has something to answer for.'

★   ★   ★

The police guard at the British Military Hospital touched his hat as he raised the barrier for us. Inside the grounds, the grey buildings were clung with ivy and had small, latticed windows.

In the reception-room we joined several other visitors who dispersed up the stairs, footsteps ringing along the shining corridors which smelt of soap and floor polish.

Robert was in a private room, lying back against his pillows with his head heavily bandaged. He looked older and more drawn than I had ever seen him look, but as we went in he opened his eyes and raised a smile.

'I thought it would be you two. I suppose Miriam is with Charles? ... It's all right. Don't bother to lie. I don't give a damn. It's nice to see you, though.'

Ian pulled a green velvet armchair from a corner and motioned me to sit down, while he asked how Robert was feeling.

'Not too bad,' Robert said with a grimace. 'It was a stupid thing to do—falling over like that. I was trying to be too clever. Ought to know better at my age.'

'I thought you said ...' Ian began.

'Oh, that!' Robert waved an impatient hand in the air. 'I was off my head. Raving. It was entirely my own fault. Are you still going to the "do" tonight?'

'Yes,' I said. 'I hope you don't mind.'

'Why should I? It'll be a cosy foursome, won't it? I'd have been the odd one out.'

'You sound like Adrian!' Ian said disparagingly. 'It wouldn't take much effort on your part to win Miriam back from that fat lecher. She knows damn well he's just a dirty old man. She's simply trying to make you see she's still attractive to someone.'

Robert grunted, a cynical smile hovering

round his lips. 'It's all very well for you to sermonise. What makes you think I want to "win her back", as you so romantically call it?'

'Then why don't you divorce her?' Ian demanded.

'I intend to do just that—as soon as this book is finished. I can't be bothered at the moment.'

'Are they looking after you in here?' I asked.

Robert managed a laugh. 'Changing the subject, Anne? How tactful of you. Yes, I'm being well looked after, except that I don't get a moment's peace, what with meals and drinks and floor-polishing and Matron's visits ... How did work go, Ian?'

Ian launched into a long and amusing description of his first day at work in Berlin and the hour's visiting time slipped away. It was well after eight when a nurse came in to draw the curtains and look pointedly at her watch.

'Will you come tomorrow?' Robert asked tiredly.

'I will,' Ian said. 'Anne's taking a few days off.'

'I was going to ask you,' I said apologetically.

Robert waved a deprecatory hand in the air. 'Don't worry about that. Look after yourself. I'll be out in about a week and then we can get on with the book. I'm not happy with it at the moment. I'll be giving it some thought while I'm here.'

The nurse pursed her lips and placed a thermometer in Robert's mouth with an air of finality. Ian and I took our leave.

'At least we know one thing ...' Ian said when we were in the car again.

'What's that?'

'Robert does know about Charles and Miriam.'

'Yes.'

'I can't understand either of them, but I suppose I don't know the whole story. There's a devil of a lot I don't understand. And you're no help. There's been something bothering *you* but you won't tell me. I feel as if I'm lost in a fog.'

'So do I,' I said. 'Ian, just be patient until I come back. I'll tell you everything then, if it's worth telling. I may just be getting everything out of perspective. I...'

'Oh, stop it!' Ian exclaimed. 'You're only worrying me more. You won't confide in me and that's that!'

He started the car with a jerky movement of his wrist and I stared out of the window, blinking back the tears. Now even Ian was being drawn inexorably from me by my own unwillingness to be truthful.

It was almost dark when he stopped the car in the forecourt of the officers' mess, and Harry Smith came striding out to meet us.

'Glad you could come,' he said warmly, clasping my hand. 'How's Robert?'

'Not too bad,' Ian replied.

We were led into a large room where tables were set around the dance floor. Most places were filled by people talking and laughing, while white-jacketed waiters flitted around dispensing drinks in the dim lighting.

Selena Smith was waving from a corner table where she sat with two other couples, plus Charles and Miriam. Introductions were performed and room was made for Ian and myself on a settee by the wall. I found myself engaged by the grey-haired lady next to me in a discussion about Robert's last-published book, and since Ian was similarly occupied in conversation, mainly by Selena, the coolness between us remained.

Dancing was already in progress and the floor was filled by whirling couples moving to the music from the band, who sat on a low dais at the far end of the room. After what seemed an eternity, Ian asked me to dance with him.

He held me loosely, so that I had difficulty in following him. When I had tripped for the third time, he said, 'I'm sorry.'

'My fault. I'm so clumsy.'

'No, I mean ... I'm sorry for what I said. I'm sorry I was annoyed.'

'I'm sorry, too, Ian. I hate to quarrel with you.'

He pulled me closer until his check rested on my hair.

'I love you,' he murmured. 'Believe me?'

'Yes.' It came out as a choked whisper.

'And you?' he asked.

'I don't know. You promised to give me time.'

I felt him sigh. 'I know. I suppose I should tell you that I won't wait for ever, but I've a feeling that I would, if I thought there was any hope.'

'There is always hope,' I said quietly, letting my hand slide up his shoulder until it rested behind his neck. I was content, at peace, warm and protected in Ian's arms. For now, that was enough for both of us.

A sumptuous buffet had been laid out in the dining-room and we all queued to fill our plates and carry them back to the ballroom. As we ate, the mood was all lightness and gaiety, probably helped by the amount of beer and spirits that had been drunk, and when the subject inevitably swung to the situation in Berlin it was taken as something of a joke. Hilarious laughter

120

greeted the most inane remarks.

'Don't tell anyone,' Smith was saying, 'but the truth about that Intelligence place is ... it's a gambling den and strip club.'

Laughing, one of the other men put in, 'You'll be telling us next they have a cabaret of sexy spies from Russia.'

'Not all from Russia,' Smith said. 'Selena's the main attraction ... Sensuous Selena and her Sexy Spies!'

A gale of laughter swept up and I was joining in it, feeling part of the joke. My own comment was, 'Adrian's been telling me he heard something in our house. He swears we're harbouring a spy ourselves.'

'It must be Miriam!' Smith said exuberantly. 'You'll have to join the group, Miriam. What shall we call you? ... Mysterious Miriam and her ... Machiavellian Minions!'

'Stop it!' Selena spluttered. 'I'm getting cramp with all this laughing.'

When I remember that night, I wince to realise the stupidity of it—the infantile mickey-taking that caused us all to howl with laughter—but that is how it was in Berlin—everything over-stated. We flung ourselves into any available joke in order to forget that outside, not so many miles away, there were Communist soldiers with guns; there were minefields; Russian jets that would 'shoot-up' the airfield for fun; and people who would risk death to get to where we were. We talked too much, drank too heartily, laughed too loudly. Berlin Madness.

I noticed Selena and Harry Smith exchange amused glances when Charles and Miriam left soon after midnight. An hour later the last waltz was played and Ian and I reluctantly made our goodbyes.

The house was in darkness when we arrived and Charles' car had gone. Ian drove into the double garage and parked the Kharmann Ghia beside the Mercedes, presenting me with my ignition key.

'What time are you leaving tomorrow?' he asked.

'Early. I want to be through Helmstedt by lunchtime.'

'Helmstedt?'

'It's the exit point from the Corridor.'

'How long will you be away?'

'Two or three days, I expect. It depends what I find to do.'

'You'll be back by the weekend?'

'I think so. Shall I send you a card while I'm away?'

In the darkness, I felt rather than saw, Ian smile as he drew me towards him.

'Yes. Say "Wish you were here", and mean it. And come back safely to me. Can I have one kiss to keep me going?'

'Just one, then,' I teased. 'It will give me

something to think about, too.'

His arms came round me loosely and his mouth found mine. My blood began to beat rapidly through my pulses as his arms tightened and I slipped my hands inside his jacket, feeling the warmth of him against me.

After a long moment, Ian laid his cheek on mine and sighed, his heart thudding loudly in my ear. He was saying my name over and over, as if no words could express his feelings.

My cheeks were wet. The strength of his emotion had found an echo in me and I was physically stirred to an alarming point, as I had never been since the collapse of my marriage.

He held me away from him, touching my hair and face. 'Are you crying?'

'A bit. I'm only flesh and blood, you know ... Oh, Ian, I want to love you. I...'

His fingers came on my lips gently, stopping the words. 'No, don't say it until you're sure. You must be sure. I want it to be for ever.'

'So do I,' I said in a low voice.

'It's late. You've got a long drive tomorrow. We ought to...'

'Ian ...' I said urgently, as I realised that this was the last time I would see him for several days and if anything should go wrong tomorrow ... 'Please, not for a few minutes yet.'

He pulled me against him roughly, covering my face with hard kisses. Unable to stop myself, I put my hands behind his head and held his mouth on mine with a longing I had never experienced.

Suddenly, Ian wrenched away and climbed out of the car. When I joined him at the garage doors he took my hand in a grip of iron.

'I didn't mean to run out on you,' he said shakily. 'I just...'

'I know,' I said softly. 'Me, too.'

*   *   *

For the second time, I waited in my room until the house was still and quiet, with the happiness of the last few hours seeping slowly away, to be replaced by a guilty fear. The house had been silent for fifteen minutes when I stole along to the study and found Alan sitting on the couch. He was wearing the blue sweater I had bought for him and looked much better for his long sleep.

He stood up and came anxiously towards me, clasping my hands in his. 'Is everything all right?'

'Yes. Don't worry.'

'You haven't changed your mind? I've been sitting here half expecting you to bring the police. I wouldn't have blamed you.'

I withdrew my hands, suddenly embarrassed by his nearness. There was a sensuous quality about him, some basic masculinity I could not help but notice. I had been roused so easily by Ian and now this man stood before me, gazing at me with hunger...

'I gave you my word,' I said, avoiding his eyes. 'I won't let you down.'

'Thank you for the sweater, and the other things. You're very kind.'

'You needed some things,' I said. 'Now, we must be as quiet as possible. We go along the veranda and down the steps. There's a small door in the side of the garage. When you're in the car the first hurdle will be over.' I didn't dare think of the other, larger hurdles facing us the next day.

In the dark stillness, broken only by the rustle of leaves in a small breeze, I crept down to the garage, with the thin shadow of the refugee behind me. The side door of the garage clicked as I opened it and Alan jumped, looking around fearfully.

'Come on!' I breathed. 'Get in the car and cover yourself with that rug. It won't be very comfortable, but you'll be safe.'

He climbed in and lay down on the front seats, wrapping the plaid rug around himself and muttering by way of farewell, 'Don't

125

forget the passports.'

'I won't,' I said. 'I'll be as early as I can.'

Closing the door gently behind me as I slipped out of the garage, I leaned for a moment against the wall, feeling the weakness of reaction. And then as I turned the corner my mouth went dry—Adrian was sitting on the bottom step.

'Adrian!' I gasped, one hand to my throat. 'What are you doing out at this time of night?'

'I've been for a walk.' He gestured towards the garage. 'I was going to ask if I could come with you, but I can see you wouldn't want me.'

'What do you mean?'

'That chap. You're going away with him, aren't you? Why didn't you meet him in town tomorrow?'

'Adrian, don't imagine things.'

'I didn't imagine *him*. I saw you come out of the study. You looked quite funny, creeping along like that.'

'It's not what you think,' I said urgently. 'Please, Adrian, I can't explain now. Don't tell anyone about this.'

'Oh, I won't. Go off on your dirty weekend.' His face contorted with sudden rage and he leapt to his feet. 'I thought you were decent. I looked up to you ... but you're as bad as my mother!' His last words were yelled as he ran away down the path.

I went after him, but when I reached the beach he had disappeared.

Why couldn't anything be simple? I thought in anguish. Everything conspired to complicate my life.

Across the lake there was an explosion as a landmine went off and I stood trembling helplessly, knowing I would never find the boy in the dark. I had no time now to worry about him. If he told Ian ... well, that would have to be explained later. Adrian himself would be sure to understand when I was free to tell him the truth. It was too much to face at this moment. It was too late. I had to get some sleep.

I turned back to the house, feeling the beginnings of a raging headache that was to plague me all night—that and the worrying.

CHAPTER SEVEN

My alarm clock sounded at five a.m. and I came awake at once, needing no reminder of what the coming day held. After dragging myself out of bed, I went to the window and pulled the curtains back to let in the pink light of dawn that was creeping from the east.

I dressed quickly, in slacks and a thick white sweater, not wanting to be over-dressed beside my companion; then I took my case down to the kitchen and made two flasks of coffee, while I wondered whether Adrian had come back last night. Perhaps I ought to ... but no, there was no time.

As I entered the garage, Alan sat up with an anxious look on his face.

'Did you sleep?' I asked.

'A little. Did you?'

'Not much.'

'If you want to back out...'

'It's too late for that,' I said, knowing it was true—if I forsook him now, leaving him to find other help in broad daylight, I could never have lived with my conscience.

'You'd better stay down until we're away from the house,' I added. 'I'll open the doors now.'

Within minutes we were on our way, driving through the lanes and then along the Heerstrasse to the city centre, with the light broadening along the sky ahead of us. I was tense with apprehension, aware that I was really on my own now. If anything should go wrong there would be no Ian, no Robert, to help me out. I had gone into this thing with my eyes wide open. Only heaven could help me now.

Beside me, the refugee sat stiffly, hands clenched between his knees. The car reeked of that stale smell of the lake which still

128

hung in his clothes, but after a while I ceased to notice it. There were other, more important things to take my attention.

The complex of roads by the Funkturm was almost deserted at this hour of the morning, except for lorries loaded with goods, and we sped on down the autobahn unhindered, towards the perimeter.

A line of articulated trucks was standing at the checkpoint waiting to go through. I drove past them and drew into the space reserved for private cars, taking my International Insurance Card and the passports into the wooden office.

The man on duty regarded me with interest. 'Going home?'

'England? No, we're just taking a few days' holiday.'

'Lucky you. Don't take more than four hours getting to Helmstedt or they'll think you've got lost. And don't do it in less than two or you'll be picked up for speeding. Have a good journey.'

I returned to the car, said, 'So far, so good,' rather grimly, and pointed the car into the half-mile no-man's land between the Allied and East German checkpoints, where the road was lined with high barbed-wire fences and the whole area overhung by huge arc lights.

A sleepy-eyed East German soldier approached us to examine the passports and the green insurance card, glancing at each of us several times. He appeared to be reading the small print on the green card, probably a ploy to make us more nervous, and he yawned as he peered inside the car; then he lifted the lid of the boot and, without a word, went inside the hut to have the documents stamped.

I got out to shut the boot and light a cigarette, hoping that I looked nonchalant. After what seemed like hours, the Vopo reappeared and gave me the papers without comment.

'Okay,' he said, and waved us on.

I drove away as fast as I dared.

'Thank God we're away from those bloody Vopos,' Alan said viciously.

'We're not away from them,' I muttered. 'We're going into their territory now. We're on our own, over a hundred miles behind the Iron Curtain, and if we miss the road we shall probably be picked up and ...' I closed my mouth, realising my nerves were showing. 'Sorry,' I added. 'You know all that, don't you?'

'Unfortunately, yes. You don't sound very happy, Anne.'

'I'm not at all happy, but it's no good ignoring the facts. Have you ever come by this road?'

'No.'

'It's quite a pleasant drive, really. Good

130

roads and open country. No towns, thank heaven. We should be all right, barring breakdowns, until we get to Helmstedt. They'll search the car there.'

'As long as they don't look too closely at me ... Can't you go faster?'

'I'm doing sixty already. It would be just great if they got us for speeding, wouldn't it?'

A few minutes later I glanced at my watch and realised that the house by the Havel would be waking now. Would Adrian tell Ian that he had seen me with a man? I shut the thoughts out. Worrying about that now would solve no problems.

The wind suddenly caught the car and I had to fight to keep it to the right side of the road; then trees closed in on either side and sheltered the car. Ahead of us, the brown body of a deer flashed across the road.

We were driving through green, hilly country. The side wind was fierce and my arms soon began to ache from the constant need to grip the wheel. When we had been travelling for an hour I stopped in a layby to pour some coffee and study the maps.

The rapidly climbing sun made the day warm and the singing of birds filled the woods and fields that lay all around us, but I could not appreciate the natural beauty. I was too aware that it was hostile country and that the biggest test was yet to come—at Helmstedt.

'Where are you heading for?' Alan asked as I handed him a cup of coffee.

'I haven't thought about it. Will you pass me that map that's in the glove compartment?'

I spread the map on the grass and knelt beside it, running my finger across it. 'Where do you want to go?'

He smiled wryly, joining me on the grass. 'You're assuming we shan't both be thrown into jail.'

'I'd rather not think about that,' I said, shivering. 'Where shall I put you off?'

'Anywhere you like. As long as I'm through Helmstedt I can manage alone. You've done enough already.'

I traced the road with my finger. 'Hanover's about fifty miles from the border. We could stop there, or ... I had thought about taking a look at the Rhine. There's an autobahn all the way to Cologne, but that's another three hundred miles. At a push, we could get there this evening.'

'Would you mind? Taking me all the way, I mean. Bonn isn't far from Cologne, is it?'

'No ... Do you want to get to Bonn?'

'Eventually. But I don't expect you to take me. I intended to hitch-hike.'

'It's illegal here,' I told him. 'I would have thought you knew that. Or don't you care? ... Anyway, since I'm going that far you might as well come with me.'

He lifted his head, looking deep into my eyes. 'Are you sure it isn't too much trouble?'

'I'll be glad of your company.'

'Will you, Anne?' He touched my hand, making it tingle, and smiled at me. 'I shall be glad to prolong our acquaintance, too.'

I stood up, folding the map, facing the journey again. 'If ...' I said. 'If we get through the next checkpoint.'

*   *   *

We reached it seventy-one minutes later—the penultimate hurdle in our grim race against Fate and the authorities. There was a feeling of squalidity and watchfulness about the place, tall pine trees interspersed with watch-towers. Huts appeared to have been flung down at random between the high wire fences and motley green uniforms adorned the stocky men who were walking about the area.

A sullen-faced Vopo took our documents into one of the huts, coming out again immediately, empty-handed, and asking us to 'Leave the car.'

Alan and I reluctantly obeyed and watched while two of the Vopos made a thorough search of the car, even looking underneath it. They were deliberately slow and I wanted to scream at them to get a move on.

At last, they moved away and the first one motioned us to return to the car. There was another long wait.

'For God's sake!' Alan muttered. 'What are they doing now?'

I didn't trust myself to reply.

Five minutes later, our Vopo came from the hut, followed by a taller officer who carried our papers. Once again we were asked to leave the car and stood on either side of it, tensely awaiting developments. The officer approached Alan, opening Robert's passport.

On the other side of the car, I felt my scalp prickle and sweat break out all over me. I hoped the soldier would not notice how white Alan's knuckles were as he gripped the top of the car door.

'You are Robert French?' came the question, with a steely glare from narrowed eyes.

Alan's back stiffened but his voice came out surprisingly assured. 'I am.'

'You write books?' the officer asked, squinting into Alan's face.

'That's right.'

'Mr French ...' He held out his hand. 'I am pleased to meet you. I find your books very entertaining.'

He shook Alan's hand, gave him the

134

passports and walked away, with his comrade at his heels. Alan glanced at me and sank into the car, letting his breath out in a huge sigh. Stifling a desire to laugh hysterically, I collapsed back into the driving seat.

'I thought we'd had it,' Alan said, running a hand through his hair.

'So did I. Let's get out of here.'

Producing the documents at the West German checkpoint beyond was a mere formality. I was dizzy with relief as I drove on to the autobahn which skirts the small town of Helmstedt—in the safety of the West.

At the first available layby I pulled in and stopped the car, to find that I was shaking.

'I can't believe it,' Alan said dazedly. 'Are we free? ... Anne, are you all right?'

I nodded, swallowing hard. 'It's only just hit me... When I think what might have happened...'

'Oh, don't! Not now! We're safe. I'm free ... I'm free!' He threw his arms around me and kissed me hard, drawing back at once and laughing. 'Sorry. I stink. It's that's filthy lake water in my clothes.'

'It smells like French perfume all of a sudden,' I said, and we both burst out laughing.

We spent an hour over lunch in a wayside café, relaxing. I was pleased that the place wasn't crowded, for the smell of Alan's clothes might have been an embarrassment, despite its being a private joke to us. Alan seemed to have come to life with the crossing of the border and we spent our time laughing and clowning.

As we drove away from the café, Alan turned to say, 'It's a hell of a long way to Bonn. Why don't you find a place to stay the night? If you still insist on taking me all the way, I can sleep in the car.'

'I'd rather stop somewhere,' I admitted. 'But you could do with a comfortable night, too. We'll take two rooms, if we can find them.'

'But I...'

'Please don't argue,' I said firmly. 'You'd be on my conscience if you had to spend another night in the car.'

We left the autobahn and drove until we found a village with a fairly large hotel perched on a hillside. They had two rooms, so we booked them and had a wash before going out to explore the countryside.

The very air smelt free and fresh and the sensation of being out in the world, accountable to no one but myself, was new and exhilarating. As we walked up the hill into the woods, the village spread out beneath us like something from Grimm's fairy tales, and the scents of summer lapped round us drowsily.

'You don't know how marvellous it is to be free,' Alan said as we paused by a stile. 'I can never thank you enough.'

'Don't try. I'm glad I was able to help.'

He took my left hand in his, turning the gold ring on my third finger. 'You're married?'

'A widow.'

'Oh, I'm sorry. How long?'

'Three years. And there's no need to be sorry.'

A puzzled frown touched Alan's brow momentarily, then he reached up to stroke my hair.

'You hair's a lovely colour—auburn lights in it ... Forgive me, but it's a long time since I was alone with a girl.'

There was a long silence as we looked into each other's eyes and his fingers moved slowly to touch my lips.

'I think I could fall in love with you,' he murmured.

'You're just grateful,' I said.

'And you are sorry for me, aren't you?'

'Yes, I suppose I am.'

'And nothing else?'

'It's difficult to say.'

He bent over me, his lips brushing mine softly, like the wings of a butterfly.

'We hardly know each other,' he said quietly, 'yet I feel that I have known you for ever. That's trite, I know. But it's true. You are totally honest, aren't you?'

'Am I?' I turned away from him, remembering Ian, with whom I had been much less than totally honest: Ian, who deserved more than I had been able to give him. I wondered dismally if I would ever feel worthy of Ian's love.

This thing with Alan, whatever it was, was an interlude and nothing more. I think we both recognised that fact. Tomorrow we would go our separate ways and probably never meet again. But today we were an island, together because of a quirk of Fate, flung into a sea of strangers. Today, and tonight, we had only each other.

We returned to the hotel and ate a leisurely dinner. From across the table Alan's eyes devoured me, making me aware of myself as a woman and of him as an attractive male. I felt strangely light-headed, not entirely because of the wine we were drinking. I even found myself wondering what it would be like if he made love to me, and such was my state that I did not shy from the thought.

It was no surprise when he came knocking softly on my door after we had gone to our separate rooms for the night. I could have stopped him, but I let him in, and went into his arms as though it had been arranged, watching in a dream as he pressed me back on the bed and snapped

138

out the light without taking his mouth from mine.

'Anne...'

'Yes?'

'Are you afraid of me?'

'No.'

He was still, lying beside me with his arms around me, and into the small, waiting silence, he said, 'I want you, Anne.'

'I know.' I was floating, drifting, off somewhere watching the couple on the bed.

I felt his hand cool on my skin beneath the nightdress. His body against mine was hard and warm. He held me tightly, kissing my eyes, my cheeks, my lips, while his hands moved gently, caressing me.

I opened my eyes. Suddenly my brain was screaming, 'Ian, Ian, Ian,' without end. It was not Alan I wanted, it was Ian. How could I go back, knowing I had ... Alan's mouth crushed down on mine, his teeth bruising me. I gasped when he let me go. Ian. Ian.

Abruptly, Alan took his hands from me and moved his body away.

'Ian?' he said.

I had not realised I had spoken the name aloud.

'Ian?' Alan said again.

Closing my eyes tightly, I felt the tears begin to overflow, running down my temples into my hair. 'Robert's brother,' I whispered.

'You love him?'

'Yes. I wasn't sure. Until now.'

'Why didn't you tell me?' he asked, a curious note of tenderness in his voice. 'I thought you were free.' He bent over me one last time, touching his lips to my cheek. 'Go to sleep now. I'm sorry.'

I stared up at the ceiling, hearing him move away, seeing the brief shaft of light that angled across the room as he left. Tears streamed down my face and I longed desperately for Ian. What was wrong with me that I could even have thought of another man?

At breakfast we said little about the previous night. Alan was gentle with me, considerate and regretful of his conduct, but I knew that it was my own fault. I should not have encouraged him. I was lucky that he was such a sensitive man or there might have been ugly consequences to my folly.

*　　*　　*

A huge suspension bridge provided passage over the Rhine and the city of Köln lay to our right. Barges, motor-boats and cruisers moved along the water and the river's banks were speckled with tents and caravans that were left behind us as we took the road for Bonn.

The federal capital was jammed with traffic that late afternoon. In the centre of the city I parked briefly by the side of the road to let Alan out.

'You'll need some money,' I said.

'No. Thank you, Anne, but you've done far too much already.'

Rummaging in my handbag, I found my purse and took out a note. 'Here. Take fifty marks, at least.'

'I won't need it.'

'Won't you? Why? Where are you going?'

'To the British Embassy.'

I stared at him, blankly. 'But I thought . . .'

'Yes, I know.' He smiled at me rather sadly. 'Anne, I can never thank you enough, but I can't explain any more. You'll probably be hearing about me soon. You'll understand then. So don't worry about it. Some day maybe I'll be able to repay you for all your kindness. Thank you again—for everything. Goodbye.'

Before I could say any more he was gone, slamming the door behind him, and was lost in the crowd. All that remained of the strange encounter was the lingering smell of lake water and Robert's passport lying beside mine in the glove compartment.

I sat still for several minutes, my thoughts darting about like bats in a cave. Why was he going to the Embassy, when he wanted to avoid the authorities? Had he been lying to me? And what did he mean by 'You'll probably be hearing about me soon'? How? In the newspapers?

It was a puzzle. The more I thought round it, the more perplexed I became. But the problem was mine no longer. I had only to wait to find out, if what Alan said was true.

Leaving Bonn behind me, I took the car ferry across the river to Königswinter, a small town nestling at the foot of vineyarded hills. There was a rack-and-pinion railway taking visitors up to the Drackenfels ruins, where there was a café with a terrace which gave a wonderful view of the river as it curved away towards the Lorelei. From the terrace I wrote a card to Ian and posted it back in Königswinter before repairing to the Gasthof for dinner.

The following day I spent on the Rhine itself, aboard one of the big Rhine cruisers that offer a seven-hour round trip of pure delight. Waiters brought crates of drink around the sun deck and the cuisine in the restaurant was superb. There was much to see on the river and along the banks, but after a while I found myself regretting that I was alone. The holiday began to pall slightly—and I began to worry.

Such a lot was going on at the house—much of which I didn't understand.

What was the truth about the papers I had found? Had Adrian really heard something? Had he been pushed into the path of that bus? What of Robert's 'accident'?

I realised guiltily that I ought to be there, in case I was needed. I had to go back. I had to tell Ian everything I knew and let him help me sort it out. Suddenly it seemed imperative.

I drove throughout the following day, stopping only for lunch in my headlong flight back to Berlin and the spider's web from which I had briefly escaped. But I felt refreshed and ready to tackle everything, which had, after all, been the point of the exercise. As I drove towards the darkening sky of the East I felt almost giddy with happiness. Ian was waiting for me. Ian! Even the checkpoints into East Germany could not dampen my spirits.

At last, a golden glow in the sky told me that I was approaching the city. I had to be careful here, for the signposts saying 'Berlin' all led to East Berlin. The final checkpoints hardly delayed me before I was driving at speed through the brightly-lit city streets. I never loved Berlin more than in those final few miles.

The lounge lights were on, warming the deep pink curtains across the window and giving the house a cosy, welcoming appearance. Leaving my case in the hall, I went into the lounge, where Miriam and Charles were on the settee. I had the impression that they had recently sprung apart.

'Oh ... hello, Anne. I thought it was Ian coming back.' She stood up, straightening her skirt and glancing at the window as lights swept across it. 'This must be him now. He's been to see Robert.'

'How is Robert?' I enquired.

'Improving. He expects to be out on Monday. How did you get on?'

'Fine, thank you. I went on the Rhine. In a cruiser.'

'Did you? How lovely.' She sounded bored by the subject, so I was not encouraged into details of my holiday.

The door flew open and Ian hurtled in, to envelop me in a bear-hug.

'Anne! Oh, it's good to see you! Are you all right?'

'Never been better,' I assured him, laughing. 'Don't squeeze me to death, though.'

He released me, grinning ruefully. 'Sorry, love. I'm a bit damp, too. It's starting to rain.'

Holding hands fiercely, we smiled joyfully at one another and I was filled with a warm sense of well-being. Now all my troubles were over.

'Has Adrian gone upstairs?' Miriam

asked, looking, surprisingly, to me for an answer.

I turned to her, bewildered. 'Adrian?'

'I do think he might have shown his face before he went up.'

'Adrian?' I said again, stupidly.

Miriam tutted irritably, waving a hand in the air. 'You've been away for four days. He didn't bother to say goodbye, so he could at least have...'

A cold hand seemed to close round my heart. In a strangled voice, I said, 'Where is Adrian?'

'He did go with you, didn't he?' Ian asked.

'No, he didn't. Do you mean ... Haven't you seen him since Monday night?'

CHAPTER EIGHT

The water from the shower was warm, like fine needles against my skin, but I took no pleasure in it. All that my mind could register was the fact—Adrian had disappeared.

I had no doubt that I was responsible for his disappearance. He had respected me and his world must have crumpled when he saw me with Alan and thought that I was like the rest. If only I had realised at the time

145

what a profound effect it would have on him ... But I hadn't. I had been too full of my own problems to give him much thought. If only I had explained to him, he might have gone with us, or at least understood why I couldn't take him. He would have been safe then. But only God knew where he was now. Four days! Alone and tortured for four days! A boy of fifteen!

Blinded by remorseful tears, I dressed and fell on my bed, weeping and accusing myself. An indefinable time later, someone came into my room and sat beside me. Ian's arms lifted me and I buried my face against his shirt.

'It's all right, darling,' he said gently. 'The police are looking for him. They'll find him before long.'

'Oh, Ian,' I sobbed. 'It's my fault. My fault!'

'Don't be silly, love. You couldn't have known.'

'I could! I should have realised.'

Ian pressed a handkerchief into my hand, saying firmly, 'Listen to me. You aren't doing any good, crying like this. You'll only make yourself ill. Dry your eyes now.'

'But it's my fault he ran away. It is, Ian.'

Taking me by the shoulders, he held me away from him. 'All right. Calm down and tell me why you think it's your fault.'

I sat up, dabbing at my eyes and plunging

thoughtlessly to the crux of the matter. 'There was a refugee.'

'What refugee?' Ian asked patiently. 'Where from?'

I stared at him for a moment, realising that I was doing it all wrong. But it was too late now. I might as well tell him the lot and get it over with.

'He came from East Germany. He swam across the Havel. I found him on Sunday night, after I had that row with Miriam.'

'Where did you find him?' This time, Ian's voice was sharper.

'On the beach. He was injured, and wet and tired. I ... put him in the study.'

Ian's eyes widened, blazing blue. 'You did what?'

'Oh, Ian, I was sorry for him. He was so thin and...'

'Yes, yes,' Ian interrupted irritably. 'So you put him in the study. Then what?'

'He wanted to get out of Berlin. So I...'

His expression was pure incredulity. 'Are you trying to tell me you ... you took him? Is that why...?'

'I did want a break—that was true. I couldn't tell you about the refugee. He begged me to keep it secret. He was desperate, Ian, and I felt responsible. I wanted to tell you, but I kept putting it off, and then it was too late. I had to trust my own judgement.'

'But ... did he have a passport?'

'No, I ... we used Robert's.'

'What?' Ian stood up and began to pace the room.

I clutched the handkerchief to me, watching Ian as he moved about, willing him to understand. 'Please don't be angry, Ian. There was nothing else I could do. And he did look a bit like Robert. It was a gamble, but luckily they didn't look too closely at Alan. I know that I ought to have told you, but...'

Ian stopped pacing. 'Alan?'

'The refugee. I called him Alan. He was English.'

He bent over me angrily. 'Have you any idea what could have happened to you? You should have turned him over to the police.'

'I know, but...'

'You were sorry for him,' Ian supplied derisively. 'Your heart's got so soft you can't think straight ... Where is he now?'

'Please don't shout at me, Ian. I left him in Bonn.' I hoped he would take me in his arms again, but he remained standing over me, anger and bewilderment written plainly on his face.

'You took him all that way?' he said incredulously. 'He must have been a very pleasant companion.'

'He was. His clothes smelt, though—from the lake. Ian ... You aren't jealous, are you?'

'Certainly not!' Ian exclaimed. 'I'm furious. Do you realise you might have been murdered or ... or anything? Why the devil did you think you could trust him?'

'Does it matter? It's all over now. I just believed in him.'

'Feminine intuition, I suppose,' Ian growled. 'And what has all this to do with Adrian?'

Fresh tears burned my eyes as I remembered the missing boy and my voice was choked. 'I took Alan down to my car on Monday night. Adrian saw us. He accused me of ... of being like his mother and then he ran off. I thought he'd come back, Ian. I didn't know ...' I buried my face in his handkerchief and at last Ian sat beside me, holding me close.

'Don't cry, darling. I'm sorry I was so angry. You must have had a terrible time.'

'I was so happy to be home,' I sobbed. 'I thought I'd be able to tell you everything and then it would be all right. But it isn't. There is no way out. Everywhere I turn there are more complications. I wish I were dead.'

'Don't talk like that!' Ian said roughly. 'That wouldn't solve anything. But in future you must tell me things. Share it all with me, Anne. I love you.'

'I know, and I love you, too.' I raised my

face and for endless seconds we did not speak, our eyes reading each other's innermost thoughts with an eloquence beyond words; then his head came down swiftly, his lips bruising my mouth. I clung to him, drowning in him, giving myself completely to the new joy of loving and being loved.

Eventually, Ian said, 'Let's not tell anyone about your refugee. I still think you must have been ...' He paused, sighing. 'Water under the bridge. Just thank God it didn't mean any trouble. As far as I'm concerned, it's Miriam's fault that Adrian has been missing so long. She should have known you would have left a note if he had gone with you.'

Even now, I hesitated to speak of my fear for Adrian's safety. This had been at the back of my mind all the time—that he really was in danger from someone who had tried once to kill him, although I still could not entirely believe it. If I told the tale and it turned out to be untrue, then both Adrian and I would look utter fools. How could I believe there was a spy in this house?

*   *   *

Miriam was alone when we went down to the lounge. She was standing by the record player, listening to one of her jazz records with her arms folded tightly.

'Charles has gone,' she said. 'He said he would drive around for a while, looking for Adrian.'

Ian snorted as he joined me on the settee. 'What good can he do? In the dark?'

'He was only trying to help,' Miriam said huffily. 'Though if Adrian wants to get lost it's his own look-out. Serve him right if he's uncomfortable.'

'Aren't you worried?' I asked.

'Not unduly. He can look after himself.' Miriam strolled to an armchair and sat down, lighting a cigarette. 'This isn't the first time something like this has happened. And he has plenty of money. He's probably gone to some hotel, trying to worry us ... When he was twelve, he had us all running round in circles for a week. But eventually he came back—he'd bought himself a runabout ticket and had been going round the Lake District.'

'I remember you rang to see if he was with me,' Ian said. 'He's an independent young devil. Don't worry, Anne. All the police have been alerted. It may take some time, but they'll find him.'

It was all very well, I thought, for them to be so sanguine, but they hadn't heard Adrian telling me of that telephone conversation, nor seen him fly almost beneath a bus. If he wasn't found by morning, I would have to tell Ian about it.

★   ★   ★

The morning sky was bright, with patches of cloud dispersing to let the sun shine through. By this time Miriam was obviously worried, though she tried not to let it show. Ian, too, was concerned, so much so that he wanted to drive round the city, not really in the hope of seeing Adrian, but for something to do.

In the Kharmann Ghia, with Ian at the wheel, we drove into the busy city centre and began cruising round the streets. The Saturday crowds were so dense that we might have passed Adrian without ever seeing him, but we felt we were helping.

'At least we know him,' I said. 'The police only have a description.'

'And a photograph. We gave them one last night ... I wonder where the young devil is?'

'I'm afraid for him,' I said.

Alerted by my tone of voice, Ian glanced at me. 'Why, darling?'

'Because ... he told me he had heard something that meant there was a spy in our house. I didn't really believe him, but...'

Ian laughed. 'That boy would imagine anything.'

'Do you think he made it up?' I asked

152

hopefully,.

'Don't you? What did he say, exactly?'

'He heard one end of a phone conversation. It was about papers and money. He wouldn't tell me any more—not even who he heard talking. He wasn't really too sure of himself. And he hinted that whoever it was had been speaking German.'

Ian sighed. 'There you are, then. Typical Adrian. He obviously thinks that spying involves papers and money. He didn't say any more because he hadn't thought of any more. Hasn't he been immersed in Ian Fleming lately? It's a day-dream, that's all.'

He sounded so sure that my own doubts faded. That incident with the double-decker had been a stupid way of making me believe Adrian's story. I wouldn't tell Ian about that because it would make him angry with the boy, who would have enough to cope with when he was found.

By lunchtime the clouds had gone and the day was so hot that the damp earth steamed under the sun. Ian and I broke off our search to return home and see if there was any news. There wasn't.

Neither Ian nor I fancied the prospect of sitting around waiting, so went out to where my car stood on the tree-shaded road. Wilhelm was coming past the garage to his own battered car in the driveway and Ian stopped for a few moments, trying out his

153

German on the gardener, who seemed amused by Ian's accent. As we stood there, a white Opel with 'POLIZEI' emblazoned on it screeched to a halt at the gates and Bracke leant out.

'We have just heard he is at the zoo,' he called. 'Are you coming with us?'

Ian and I ran to the police car. As I climbed in, Ian turned to Wilhelm, who stood gaping on the driveway.

'Wilhelm, tell Mrs French where we've gone, will you?'

The gardener nodded. '*Jah, jah*. Okay,' and hurried to the front door.

The police car roared away, with its blue light winking and two-tone horn blaring out a warning.

'We heard over the radio,' Bracke said. 'I was going to my house for a meal.' He turned to the driver, urging him to go faster, before speaking again over his shoulder. 'A boy answering to Adrian's description was seen, but they lost him. A day like this, there are hundreds of people at the zoo. My men will cover all the exits and there will be others searching for him. We will find him.'

The car sped on. All the other traffic had to stop, by law, at the sound of the siren, and the white car flashed along the middle of the roads, often with barely room to spare between the lanes of stationary cars. Down the wide Heerstrasse we screamed:

154

round Theodor Heuss Platz, seemingly on two wheels, with white, staring faces turned to us from car windows and pavements. It seemed as though the city stood still.

The police car swung giddily round Ernst Reuter Platz and within minutes we were at the Zoological Gardens, being greeted by a uniformed policeman at the gate.

'He has not come out yet,' Bracke told us as we entered the zoo. 'You go that way. I go this.'

Hand in hand, Ian and I ran past the grotesque statue of a gorilla, leaving the aquarium building towering to our right, until Ian drew up, panting.

'It's no good running. We shall wear ourselves out and we can't look properly.' So we began to walk, looking to left and right as we searched the crowds, everything but the need to find Adrian forgotten.

The zoo was a maze of small paths running around the open areas, where the animals were kept behind dry moats, and twining through trees and lawns and flower-beds. There were thousands of people, but no sign of the tall, dark-haired boy we sought. On the stage of the Concert Garden a band was playing, of all things, Strauss Waltzes, for the enjoyment of the people sitting at tables beneath sunshades.

The sound of children's voices came from a play park. Opposite, a small boy was throwing cherries across the rail and ditch which separated him from a growling black bear.

At the birdhouse we passed into darkness and then into the humidity of tropical foliage and bright, fluttering wings. Outside again, we encountered Bracke.

'No sign of him?' he asked. 'Ach, we must be missing him by seconds.'

Ian and I pushed on, through a sea of unfamiliar faces. The elephants were being hosed down, which would have been an amusing spectacle at any other time. Then, we were too busy scanning the crowd.

On the edge of a lake, pink flamingoes were being fed, watched by a jostling crowd—but not Adrian. We went through the stench of the cat-house and emerged gratefully into the fresh air.

'Can we have a minute's rest?' I asked. 'I'm worn out. Wouldn't it be simpler to wait at the gate?'

'Yes,' Ian said doubtfully. 'I suppose it would. Do you want to sit down for a while?'

'Yes. No. Oh, Ian, I can't. I'm so afraid for him.'

'I'm not,' Ian said grimly. 'Wait till I get my hands on that young blighter.'

We walked on, slowly, and soon encountered the *Oberkommissar* again. He was puffing with exertion and more red-faced than ever as he pulled out a handkerchief to mop his glistening brow.

'He must be avoiding us,' he said irritably. 'He must know we are searching for him ... It is so hot!'

I threw back my head, shaking the heavy hair from my neck, where it was sticking, and as I did so I gasped, pointing.

'Up there! Look!'

All heads turned to the roof of the aquarium building, several floors high. Adrian was standing near the edge, his orange shirt seeming to shout against the blue sky.

Bracke set off at a run, with Ian and myself at his heels, but Adrian saw us and moved out of sight. At the door of the aquarium, Bracke pushed the ticket collector aside, shouting, *'Polizei!'* and shouldered his way through the crowds to the stairs, dashing up two at a time. I would have followed, but Ian held me back.

'Don't go up, darling.'

'But I must, Ian. He'll come down if he sees me. Or you—you go.'

Ian looked anguished. After a moment, he said, 'We'll both go.'

It was a struggle to break through the knots of people standing gaping on the stairs. We had reached the second floor when we met Bracke coming down.

He hurried past us, saying, 'He's

jumped,' and thundered on down the stairs.

'Oh, God!' Ian breathed.

'Ian!' I whispered. 'He's not...'

Still shouting '*Polizei*!' Bracke pushed his way through the emergency exit into the street. A wide-eyed crowd had gathered. As I came through the door, Bracke was bending over Adrian, who lay sprawled on the ground. Ian prevented me from rushing forward.

'Why, Ian?' I asked in anguish. 'Why did he jump?'

Bracke glanced round, moved away.

And then I saw the knife in Adrian's back.

CHAPTER NINE

Miriam was in the garden, picking roses. She looked round as Ian and I came on to the patio, beginning to walk quickly, eagerly, towards us.

'I thought you'd got lost as well,' she said. 'Where is he?'

She paused, seeing our faces. Ian was white beneath his tan and my own face was streaked with tears.

Miriam began to tremble. 'What...?'

'Come and sit down.' Ian took her arm, leading her to the settee, where she sat down stiffly, her face blank with apprehension. Ian crouched in front of her.

'Miriam ... Adrian...'

'He's dead?' Miriam managed to whisper.

'I'm afraid so.'

A stifled sob escaped me, but Miriam simply sat, staring down at the roses on her lap, while her face slowly assumed the yellow colour of the flowers. Her hands were slowly crushing the roses, petals falling unnoticed on to the floor.

She looked up at Ian, her eyes unfocused. 'Are you sure?'

'We saw him.' His voice was infinitely gentle and sad. 'He fell from the roof of the aquarium.'

Her hands, I saw, were spotted with blood where the rose thorns had entered her flesh, but she went on crushing the flowers.

'He always did like fishes,' she said in a quick, brittle voice. 'And animals. The zoo is his favourite place.'

Numbly, I leaned forward and tried to take the roses from her, but she brushed me aside as she stood up.

'I'll put these flowers in water. They won't last long in this heat.'

'Miriam ...' Ian said worriedly, getting to his feet.

'It's all right, Ian. I'm fine. I'll ask Eleonore to make coffee. You must be very thirsty.'

Watching her through a misty veil of tears, I realised with sad surprise that Miriam had loved her son far more than she had appeared to.

'Go with her, Anne,' Ian said quietly. 'Is there a doctor I can phone?'

'Yes. Dr. Meister. He's in the notebook.'

Miriam had gone into the kitchen and was filling a vase with water. Her hand was surprisingly steady. Eleonore was waiting behind her with the kettle and looked at me with questioning eyes. Seeing my tears, she breathed, *'Nein!'*

I nodded. Eleonore dropped the kettle and burst into noisy tears which Miriam ignored as she turned with the vase in her hand.

'Adrian will like these flowers,' she said. She sounded breathless and her voice was too light to be normal. As she arranged the crushed roses in the vase, petals showered on to the table until the stalks were nearly bare.

'Come and lie down,' I suggested, intensely worried by her manner.

'Good idea,' said Ian from the doorway.

Miriam sighed. 'Very well. I didn't sleep much last night. I wish Robert were here.'

She allowed me to take her to her room, but she wouldn't lie down. She sat on her bed until the doctor arrived.

The small, spare Doctor Meister had

obviously been informed of the situation by Ian, who came with him. The unresisting Miriam was given an injection and gently forced into a supine position with the coverlet over her.

'Are you the husband?' the doctor asked of Ian.

'No. He's in hospital.'

'So? He is told?'

'Not yet.'

'*Frau* French will wish to tell him, I think. She will sleep now, but later ... she may feel well enough to go to her husband.'

Behind them, Miriam gave a great sobbing sigh and relaxed into sleep.

'Good,' the doctor said. 'You will go with her, *naturlich*?'

'Yes, of course,' Ian replied.

The doctor looked to where I was leaning against the door. 'And it will be good for another lady to go also. Your wife is well enough?'

Not bothering to correct his error, I nodded. 'Yes, I'll go.'

When Ian showed the doctor out, I followed them as far as the study, where I stood staring out of the window, knowing only that Adrian had run away because of me. Now he was dead, which was also my fault. Why had he been killed? I asked myself over and over again, fighting to see through the mental block that had descended on my memory the minute I saw that knife, and the blood...

'Why don't you try to sleep, darling?' Ian asked as he came up behind me.

'I couldn't.'

His arms came round me, cradling me. 'Don't blame yourself.'

'How can I help it? I sent him to his death.'

'Don't say that!' Ian said sharply.

Turning, I pressed my face against him. 'Oh, Ian, who did it? Why didn't Bracke see someone else on the roof?'

'It took time for us to get into the aquarium. The ... the murderer slipped off the roof and joined the gaping crowds before Bracke got up there. It must have been a madman. There's no reason for anyone to hurt Adrian.'

'I keep thinking I should know something—something that would explain ... but the more I think about it, the more confused I feel.'

'Of course you do. You've been through a lot lately. You've got to rest. I don't want two invalids on my hands. Come on.'

I lay with my eyes closed, while the events of the past week whirled through my mind like a broken jig-saw puzzle. If only I could fit the pieces together, remember things in sequence ... but my mind refused to co-operate. Half-awake, I began to dream...

A shadow outside the darkened study turned into Alan, who was holding a paper. Eleonore came from somewhere and took the paper, falling, as she did so, into the lake where Robert floated unconscious. Adrian's head appeared, laughing. Then Charles was coming towards me, with Miriam having hysterics in the background, but Ian hit Charles and he fell into the arms of a Vopo who had somehow got hold of the paper and waved it as he advanced on Ian, brandishing a knife. When I tried to stop him I found myself fighting through a sea of white faces in the middle of which was a blurred outline of someone I ought to know, but couldn't identify...

My eyes flew open. I had seen that face somewhere ... at the zoo. In the aquarium! I had turned, to follow Bracke down the stairs, and glimpsed that face among the crowd. Who was it? I had to remember. But I couldn't.

When I closed my eyes again, some healing mechanism brought sleep, and the next thing I knew Ian was giving me a cup of tea and telling me it was time to go to the hospital.

Miriam was up and dressed in a navy-blue suit and white gloves. She had drawn her hair into the unflattering bun she favoured and her face was ravaged despite the absence of tears.

When we reached the hospital, we found Robert sitting up in bed and looking more like his old self, but he frowned when he saw his wife.

'What's wrong?'

'We've brought some bad news,' Ian said gravely, pulling up a chair for Miriam.

Robert took a deep breath and squared his shoulders. 'Well?'

Staring down at her gloves as she twisted them in her hands, Miriam said flatly, 'Adrian is dead.'

I heard Robert draw a sharp breath, his gaze fixed incredulously on his wife's bent head. After a moment he exclaimed, choking. 'What? Adrian? He can't be.'

In the same expressionless voice, Miriam said, 'He was stabbed. You tell him, Ian.'

Ian took up the story, as briefly as was possible, and all the time Robert stared disbelievingly at his wife. When Ian stopped talking, Robert poured himself a glass of water and drank it down, replacing the glass with a thud. He sat looking into space, hands clutched tightly and beads of perspiration standing out on his brow.

'Bracke called just before we came out,' Ian said. 'There were no fingerprints on the knife.'

'How did Bracke get into this?' Robert demanded.

'It was him I first went to, when we knew Adrian was missing. He took a personal interest after that.'

'I see.' Robert's face was grey. He closed his eyes and rubbed at them with the heels of his hands.

The silence had become almost tangible when Miriam slowly raised her head and spoke again in a voice that was almost inaudible.

'Robert ... can you forgive me? I ... I should have known sooner. I just thought...'

Robert sighed and said quietly, 'Do you ever think?' His hands fell back on to the sheets and his eyes were bleak. 'Except about yourself ... and your men friends?'

A tear trickled slowly down Miriam's cheek. 'Oh, Robert, what happened to us? I know I deserve to be punished, but surely this is punishment enough? Our son, Robert...'

'Your son,' Robert said harshly. 'He was not my child. I knew that, but I accepted him, hoping that I could forgive you—but I could never forget.'

Miriam stared at him, her green eyes liquid and expressionless. 'He *was* yours! He *was*! He was so like you.'

'Of course he was. He was my brother's son, wasn't he?'

Miriam's lips moved, making an

165

inarticulate sound.

'My brother,' Robert repeated. 'I know he visited you at the house. I suspected, but I could never prove anything.'

'There was nothing to prove,' Miriam said listlessly. 'Chas and I were friends, but he was your brother and I loved you. I swear to you, Robert, Adrian could only have been your son.'

Robert lay back and turned away from her. 'Get out! Go back to Ellistone.'

She sat still for a moment; then she stood up with quiet dignity, ignoring the tears which were flowing down her face and dripping on to the front of her jacket. She opened her mouth to say something to Robert, but decided there was nothing more to be said at that moment, and slowly turned towards the door with her head held high.

'Robert ...' Ian said.

Robert waved his arm tiredly. 'Go away. Leave me alone.'

The sound of our footsteps along the corridor seemed to reverberate inside my head as we walked away from that room.

'All these years,' Ian said, as if thinking aloud. 'All these years he's hated her for something she didn't do. He's ruined her life *and* Adrian's.'

'Maybe this ... this terrible thing will bring them together,' I said.

'Maybe, though it hardly seems worth Adrian's life to make Robert see reason.'

Miriam was sitting calmly in the back of the Mercedes. The fingers which held her cigarette trembled slightly, but she had wiped the tears from her face.

'I can't tell you how sorry I am about that,' Ian said, turning to look at her over the seat. 'It was bad enough for you having to tell him, without all those accusations.'

'It's my own fault,' Miriam said in a low voice. 'You see, I've never told him the truth before. It is the truth, but I can't expect him to believe it.'

'Why not?'

'Because ... soon after I became pregnant with Adrian, Robert and I had a terrible quarrel—about his work, as always. He shouted at me. He said if I was so dissatisfied I should find someone else. I said, "How do you know I haven't?" ... Robert must have thought ... well, Chas was visiting us regularly at that time, and ... well...'

'Let's go home, Ian,' I said quietly.

*   *   *

Miriam went to bed as soon as we reached the house and Ian and I sat opposite one another in the lounge, drinking coffee and hardly speaking. I had still not remembered

167

who it was that I had seen at the zoo, but my memory was slowly returning about previous events.

I looked across at Ian, who was filling his pipe.

'Ian...'

He raised his head. 'Yes?'

'I'm sure Adrian must have heard something. It's the only explanation. I'm sure he was telling the truth.'

'What makes you so sure?'

'The fact that he's been ... killed.'

Ian sighed. 'All right, then. For the sake of argument, let's suppose he did hear something. Who could it have been?'

'Anybody,' I said helplessly.

'Quite. And did he tell anyone other than you?'

'I don't think so. It was our secret, he said.'

'So who else could have known?'

'Maybe the person he overheard saw him and ... I don't know.'

'This,' said Ian, 'is going into the realms of wild fantasy. Darling, you aren't thinking logically.'

'It looks that way, I know, but I'm still certain he did hear something, because ... when we were in town last Monday he was pushed into the road. He was almost killed then. The bus only just missed him.'

'He was pushed?'

168

'He said he was.'

'Exactly. He said. Did you see it happen?'

'No, but the crowd...'

'It was more of his game, that's all, the stupid idiot!'

'I had thought of that, but ...' I was almost in tears. I took a cigarette from my packet and lit it with shaking fingers as Ian came to sit beside me.

'You're overwrought, darling. Can you really see anyone in this house trying to kill Adrian?'

I shook my head miserably.

'Drink your coffee,' Ian instructed. 'And stop thinking about it. The police will find out what happened.'

'Do you think I should tell them about Alan?'

'Only if they ask. Don't volunteer the information ... Look, it's getting late. We could both do with some sleep. Do you want a sleeping pill? I've got some in my room.'

I climbed to the second floor, where the guest room was, and waited outside while Ian fetched the tablet. As he came back there was a sound from the box-room and with a glance at me Ian opened its door.

Miriam was in there, kneeling on the floor as she quietly packed away the electric train set. She did not look up as Ian went in to her.

'Miriam ...' he said quietly.

'Don't stop me, Ian. He won't need this any more. I had to do it. It was Adrian's. It's all I have.' She bent her head and began to weep silently.

Ian bent and eased her to her feet. 'Do it tomorrow. Sleep now.'

Miriam picked up one of the engines and hugged it to her as she accompanied me back to her room, where she let me help her to undress. She lay beneath the sheets, clutching the engine to her breast, and when I turned out the light she spoke my name.

'Anne. Thank you.'

Tears filled my eyes as I closed the door and turned into the comfort of Ian's arms.

Having taken the sleeping tablet with a glass of water, I went to bed, but I could not shut out the sight of Adrian, lying still and smashed on the concrete, with blood soaking his orange shirt around the wooden handle of the murder weapon. And a face in the crowd...

As sleep overcame me, I heard the boy's voice, excited and full of mystery. 'I know there's a spy in the house, and I know who it is, but I'm not saying.'

I turned over. Out of the mists swirling in my mind, I heard my own voice, surrounded by laughter, saying lightly, 'Adrian's been telling me he heard something in our house.'

170

Of course! That was the answer. He *had* heard something! And *I* had told them!

I sat up and switched on the bedside light, my memories clicking into place at last.

It had been a joke, of course. Everyone had laughed. But someone had not thought it funny. Who could that someone have been? Miriam? Selena? Harry? Charles? Yes, Charles had been there. And Charles had put the papers in the study, had he not? Had he realised that one paper was missing? Had he searched my room?

I leapt out of bed to search feverishly among my underclothes in the drawer of the dressing-table. The lavender sachet was still there, the paper still safely inside it.

Fuzzy-headed from the effects of the sleeping tablet, I stumbled back to bed and tripped over the white fur rug. As I fell to my knees, grabbing the end of the bed, something caught my eye—a piece of paper just visible behind the bedside cabinet, probably blown there by the wind. I crawled forward and pulled it out.

It was an envelope, sealed. On the front, in blotchy ink, was written: Mrs H. It was a sprawling, ill-formed handwriting which I instantly recognised—as Adrian's.

CHAPTER TEN

I had dragged myself into bed and fallen into oblivion at once. When I awoke, the bedside light was still on and the clock showed almost ten.

Remembering the envelope, I pulled out the single piece of exercise paper. The note read:

> *Tuesday. I have to see you as soon as you get back. Something else has happened and I daren't stay in the house. Don't trust anyone. I'll be at the* bockwurst *stall on the corner of the Pickelsdorferstrasse every night at eight. Please come. I must talk to you. Adrian.*

So he had come back to the house—at least long enough to deliver the note. I stared blankly into the distance, thinking of the boy waiting vainly for me.

A knock on the door startled me and I pushed the note back into the envelope, putting it beneath my pillow before going to open the door.

'How are you?' Ian asked.

'Better. I'll be all right. You?'

'I'm okay. The police are here. Miriam and I have talked to them and Eleonore's in there now. They want to see you. And I'm

172

just off to fetch Robert. He phoned to say he was coming out today instead of tomorrow. Wants to be here, I suppose.'

'Can I talk to you a minute?'

He glanced at his watch. 'Not now, darling. They're waiting for you and I have to go. I won't be long.'

When I went downstairs shortly after this, I found Bracke waiting in the hall. His red face was grave.

'Good morning, Mrs Holbrook. In here, please.'

In the dining-room, two green-uniformed police officers sat at the table. The younger one was writing on a notepad, while the other twiddled a pen in his fingers as he motioned me into a chair.

'Mrs Holbrook? I am *Kommissar* Schneider. This is my colleague, *Obermeister* Wagner.'

As I sat down, I was aware of Bracke standing by the closed door behind me. *Kommissar* Schneider smiled, regarding me with friendly brown eyes as he established my relationship to the family and asked about my movements of the last few days. I managed to avoid mentioning the refugee.

At last came the question, 'Can you suggest any reason why Adrian French should be murdered?'

I hesitated, licking my suddenly dry lips. 'I ... he told me he had heard someone

173

talking on the telephone and that he knew there was a spy in the house.' I turned to glance at Bracke, but he appeared impassive.

'Did you believe him?' Schneider asked.

'Not at first, no.'

'What had he heard?'

'Something about papers and money. That was all he would tell me.'

Bracke asked, 'Did he say *who* he heard?'

'No.'

'Did you tell anyone about this?' Schneider continued.

'I did, but it was meant as a joke. I thought he was imagining things.'

'Who did you tell?'

I listed the names of the people who had been at our table that Monday night and ended by handing over the note from Adrian. Schneider read it through and handed it to Bracke.

'So,' Schneider said. 'He was afraid.'

'Yes, and ... there was something else that made me wonder ... When Adrian and I were in town, he was pushed into the road.'

Schneider's eyes widened. 'Tell us all about it, please.'

So I repeated it, haltingly, in as much detail as I could remember, explaining my own thoughts about it as I went. When I had finished, I was dismissed, though they asked to see Miriam again.

Relieved to have that over, I went into the lounge, where Miriam was dusting her precious china.

'The police would like another word with you,' I said.

She turned, a bone-china cup in her hand. 'Oh, would they?' Her voice was flat, her eyes glassy, and she absent-mindedly gave me the cup as she came past.

Replacing the cup in the cabinet, I closed the glass door and sat down in an armchair, opening a magazine without the slightest desire to read. A few minutes later the doorbell rang and when I went to answer it I was astonished to find Charles Ellistone on the doormat. Hadn't the man any tact or decency?

'Good morning,' he said stiffly. 'Is Mrs French in?'

I stepped back. 'You'd better come in.'

Miriam, who came from the dining-room at that moment, stopped in her tracks when she saw Charles, with a look of blank amazement.

'Good morning,' he said again, but Miriam made no response.

From behind her, Bracke said, 'Ah, Mr Ellistone, you have saved us the trouble of finding you. Would you come in here for a moment?'

Charles frowned. 'Yes, of course. What's

175

going on? Miriam, are you well?'

'Yes, thank you,' she said tersely, giving him a look which made him flinch.

'What does he want?' Miriam said to me as we went back into the lounge.

'He didn't say. Perhaps he's come to offer his condolences.'

'How could he know? I haven't contacted him since yesterday.'

'Oh ... then he doesn't know about...'

Miriam clenched her hands. 'I'd give anything to see his face when they tell him.'

Her remark about contacting Charles had sent me off on another train of thought. As she went to sit down, I said thoughtfully, 'Miriam ... Did you tell anyone that Adrian was at the zoo? After we'd gone, I mean.'

She paused in the act of lighting a cigarette. 'The police asked me that. Yes, I phoned Charles to tell him and as soon as I put the phone down it rang again and it was Selena, so I told her. And she would tell Harry. I was so pleased I would have told anyone. Eleonore knew almost at once, of course.'

I dropped into a seat, thinking furiously. So Charles was involved again! He could have reached the zoo and found Adrian before we did. But that meant ... I stared at Miriam. What had she meant by 'I'd give anything to see his face when they tell him'? Did she think that Charles had killed

176

Adrian? Was she even now wondering if he were a good enough actor to feign surprise?

A car drew up in the driveway. At the same moment, Charles came into the lounge. Ignoring him, Miriam went to the window.

'It's Robert and Ian,' she said. 'I'll let them in.'

I thought Charles looked dazed. He moved slowly to a chair and flopped down in it, shaking his head, muttering, 'I can't believe it.'

When the front door opened, I went to greet Robert. He was pale and his forehead was still plastered, but he was smiling.

As soon as he had had a cup of coffee, Charles excused himself, obviously feeling uncomfortable.

'Come back and see us this evening,' Robert invited.

On his way to the door, Charles paused uncertainly. 'I, er, don't want to ... be in the way.'

'Nonsense,' Robert said. 'You would have come under normal circumstances. We must carry on as usual.'

*   *   *

It was not until after lunch that I had a chance to speak to Ian alone. I had gone to my room, ostensibly to tidy up, and he came to find me.

'Do you still want to talk to me?' he asked.

'Yes. Come in, Ian, and close the door. You can sit on the bed if you like.'

He sat, with a bemused expression on his face. 'What is it now?'

'I had a note from Adrian—you can't see it. I've given it to the police. He said something else had happened. That's why he stayed away. He was afraid. You see, he *did* know something.'

'Anne ...' Ian said wearily. 'Let's not go into all that again.'

'We must. It's important, Ian. He wasn't playing games.'

Ian sighed and put his head in his hands. 'So. You think it was true. In which case, you think someone we know killed Adrian. Not very likely, is it?'

'On the surface, no. But why is Bracke taking such an interest? He's not with the Criminal Police—he's Counter-Intelligence. Adrian told me that Bracke was out on the lake when we were, watching us. I scoffed at him, but now I wonder.'

Ian was looking at me thoughtfully. 'If anyone else told me all this, I'd think they were crazy.'

'I know it sounds crazy. That's why I wanted to talk to you. But Adrian *has* been murdered. There must be something in it.'

'Yes, I suppose so.' He sounded tired and disinterested.

Determined to carry this through now that I had begun, I took my lavender sachet from the drawer and snipped at the stitches until I could remove the paper, which I gave to Ian.

His attention sharpened as he read the document and when he looked up at me I saw that I had reached him.

'Where did you get this?'

I told him, with many interruptions, of Miriam's phone call to Charles, of the shadow on the veranda, and of my consequent search of the study.

'Why didn't you tell me about this before?' he demanded.

'I was going to, but I didn't get the chance, and I wasn't absolutely sure I'd heard right. Then I did talk to Robert about it. Ask him, if you like. But he didn't seem to believe they would really do anything. He said Charles was only trying to keep Miriam sweet by pretending to go along with the plan. And when nothing happened I assumed he had been right. What with the refugee and everything, I'd completely forgotten about this paper until last night.'

'You think Adrian heard Miriam on the phone?'

'It's the most likely explanation, isn't it?'

'None of it sounds likely,' Ian said

179

angrily. 'If you're so sure, we ought to take this paper to Bracke.'

'Oh, but ... that's just it. I'm not sure. I've no proof, have I? But if we could somehow show Charles that we know about it, and...'

'You want me to accuse him of murder?'

'No! Ian, don't keep growling like that. You said you would help me. If we show Charles that paper ... maybe everything else will come out. We'll all be there. He can't hurt all of us.'

Ian shook his head. 'I still don't like it.'

'Then I'll do it myself,' I said bitterly. 'Forget I ever asked you.'

He looked up at me, a spark of amusement in his eyes. 'You're just stubborn enough to try it, too ... All right. I'll go along with it for the moment.' He stood up, putting the paper in his pocket, and held out his hands. 'Let's take a walk somewhere.'

★   ★   ★

When I was changing for dinner, I found myself trembling with apprehension, wondering what the evening would bring. Had Adrian lied to me? Was his death coincidental? What was the truth about the paper? What would Charles do?

As I went down the stairs, Ian came in by

180

the front door, explaining that he had left something in the car, and we joined Robert and Miriam in the dining-room.

As we returned to the lounge, Miriam asked, 'Why did you tell Charles to come tonight?'

'Because he's a lonely soul,' Robert replied. 'Don't you want to see him?'

Miriam shuddered. 'I wish I never had to set eyes on him again.'

Ian raised his eyebrows expressively at me but said nothing.

We talked about nothing that is worth recounting. I found myself giving a lengthy account of my trip, without mentioning Alan, of course, talking far too much in my nervousness. Every part of me was tensed, waiting for the doorbell to announce Charles's arrival.

When it did ring, I was filled with terror and wished that I had destroyed the paper. But the mystery had to be solved.

Outside, it was growing dark. The scent of roses drifted into the room on a warm breeze and only the tall lamp by the french windows illuminated the room. It should have given the place a cosy atmosphere, but for me it was gloomy and too full of shadows.

Since we could not immediately tackle Charles—it had to be handled carefully— time slid by in desultory conversation. Ian was uneasy, fidgeting in his chair and fiddling with his pipe, and it seemed strange that the other three could talk so naturally, despite the obvious constraint between Miriam and Charles.

Then the guns beyond the perimeter began to fire spasmodically.

'Damn Russians!' Charles muttered. 'Why don't they go back where they belong?'

Robert laughed shortly. 'Come off it, Charles. The East Berliners wouldn't know what to do with themselves if they were left alone.'

'Robert!' Miriam reproved. 'You mustn't make fun of them. Those poor people.'

'Yes, yes, I know. I was just rambling, my dear. But I can't see the Russians, or the Allies, leaving this place for a long time yet.'

'Especially,' Ian put in, looking pointedly at Charles, 'when they have so many agents willing to help them.'

Charles sat upright—like a man with an uneasy conscience, I thought—and was silent for a full half-minute before spluttering, 'Agents?'

'Spies, then,' Ian amended in a hard voice. 'You ought to know all about that, Ellistone.'

'Me? Me?' Charles gasped. 'Why ... How ... Why should I know?'

'Who better?' Ian said. 'Aren't you one of

them? And for the lowest motive imaginable.'

Charles leaned forward, glaring at Ian. 'Do you realise I could have you for slander? In front of witnesses, too.'

Slowly, Ian took the fateful paper from his pocket and unfolded it. 'What about this, then? Anne found it in the study—after you took the rest of the documents back. What made you change your mind? You copied those papers. Why didn't you leave them?'

Charles sat, blinking owlishly with his mouth open.

Miriam gasped. 'Ian! He didn't...'

'May I see that paper?' Robert asked.

Ian handed it over. 'He didn't what, Miriam?'

Her eyes were wide. 'He didn't get any papers. He said it was impossible. When I went to meet him...'

'Of course it was impossible,' Charles blustered. 'I told you there was only a faint hope.'

'Faint hope!' Miriam spat. 'You never intended to do anything. It was just a trick, to make me think you were sincere,. I realised that. What kind of a fool do you take me for?'

'Miriam!' Charles said painedly.

She leaned towards him, green eyes flashing. 'Don't lie to me. You never intended to marry me.'

'You shouldn't be so gullible,' Robert said roughly.

Charles turned on Ian. 'So what do you mean—after I took the documents back? There never were any documents.'

'Then what were you doing out on the veranda that night?' I demanded. 'And don't say it wasn't you. I saw you. And where was your jacket that night, when I met you upstairs? You'd taken it off because it was soaked!'

'When was this?' Miriam asked, staring at me blankly.

'The night after the party,' Ian supplied. 'The night of the storm. The night before we went to East Berlin—when Robert was supposed to be picked up with those papers on him.'

Miriam went slightly pale and frowned. 'Charles had a button come off his jacket. I was sewing it on for him. He didn't leave the room, except once, and that was only to go to the bathroom.'

'Of course I didn't, Charles said hoarsely. 'Don't know what they're talking about.'

'All right, that's enough!' Robert said harshly. 'I won't have any more unpleasantness in my house. If Charles and Miriam want to row they can go outside. And you two can go and throw stones if you wish ... As for this stupid paper ... Anyone

184

could have made it up—even Adrian. I've never heard such a lot of hysterical nonsense.'

'Nonsense?' Ian exclaimed. '*Some*one was out on the veranda that night. And that paper...'

'Were you there?' Robert asked.

'No, but Anne says...'

Robert looked at me. 'Well, Anne?'

'It's true. I told you about it.'

'You didn't tell me about this paper.'

'At the time I didn't think it was important. You laughed off the idea of a plot against you, so I...'

'I might not have done if you had shown me this paper. But you didn't. Did you have it then? Are you sure it was that night you found it? With so much happening it wouldn't surprise me if you've made a mistake. Perhaps you found it some other day—when Adrian could have left it around.'

'But I didn't. I remember distinctly...'

Robert glanced at his brother. 'I'm sorry, Ian, I know you were convinced about this, but you haven't been here long enough to understand the full situation. This city does strange things to people. A great many women can't stand it, especially the imaginative ones like Anne. Her mind's been playing tricks. I've seen it happen before. A lot of service wives have to be sent

185

home to avoid a breakdown. Ask Harry Smith about it.'

'Are you saying I imagined the whole thing?' I gasped. I turned to Ian, who was staring at me. 'You think so, too, don't you? You all think I'm mad!'

Charles drained his glass, cleared his throat loudly and made excuses to leave. Nobody tried to stop him.

'I didn't imagine it!' I insisted.

'You have had a rough time,' Miriam said. 'What Robert says is quite true—I've heard Selena talking about the problems they have with some Army wives. Why don't you go and lie down?'

'Ian!' I cried, turning to him for help now, when I needed it most.

But Ian only gazed at me with concern as he took my hand.

'Darling, of course you aren't mad. But this whole thing has come from you. No one else knows anything...'

'Except Adrian, who is dead!' I said. I looked round at them, in turmoil. Everyone had turned against me.

'Adrian's death,' Robert said patiently, 'has nothing to do with this. He was killed quite without motive. He must have been. There is no other explanation.'

Ian stood up, pulling me with him. 'You must go to bed and rest, darling. You'll feel better in the morning. It's been a hell of a day for us all.'

Stunned, I allowed myself to be led to my room.

'Can you manage alone?' Ian asked gently.

'Don't humour me!' I cried, twisting away from him. 'I thought I could depend on you, but you've let me down as well.'

'Darling...'

'Don't call me that! You don't love me, or you would believe me.'

Ian flung the door open and picked me up, depositing me on the bed. 'I do love you. If you're ill, I want you to be well. Sleep on it and we'll talk in the morning.'

'Go away!' I snapped. 'I'll sort it out myself. All your talk about sharing things ... I was self-reliant before you came along and I can be self-reliant again.'

'Anne, don't...'

'Just leave me alone.'

He bent to kiss me but I moved away. 'Don't touch me!'

Ian was hurt. I knew it, but I made no attempt to stop him as he left me alone. I was filled with blind rage.

So I was imagining things, was I? I suppose I had typed the paper out myself, had I? Oh, if only I had let Ian take it to Bracke ... now Robert would doubtless destroy it—the one tangible clue in the whole puzzle.

187

I felt that I had the key. Locked in my brain was the answer. I sat holding my head, as if by doing so I could collate my thoughts.

At last I realised ... of course—the face at the zoo! I must remember whom I had seen, as Bracke rushed past down the stairs. Concentrating on this one thought, I went out on to the veranda and slowly down the steps. The face. The face. Who?

The light from the lounge fell softly across the lawn and sleeping flowers. The shrubs were wet with dew and a mist hung low over the lake, glowing eerily in the moonlight. When I reached the beach I heard the rustling of reeds at the edge of the lake and recalled that it was not far from here that I had met Alan, exactly a week ago—a week in which I had run the gamut of emotions. Despite this, I was sure that my mental faculties were as stable as they had ever been. I, and I alone, had the answer to the mystery, and it stemmed from one thing—the face at the zoo.

I tried to picture the scene in the aquarium—the crowded stairs; the jostling people, staring; Bracke dashing past, saying, 'He's jumped!' I had turned to follow Bracke and seen ... My racing memories stopped, congealing into that one point of time. The face ... yes, I could see it quite clearly. Among the trees, there it

188

was—white in the moonlight. The face I had seen at the zoo! I came to an abrupt halt.

The face seemed to be disembodied. Then the man stepped forward, towards me.

'Good evening, Mrs Holbrook.'

'Wilhelm!' I cried. 'It was you...'

For another split second I stood motionless, suddenly realising my danger; then my muscles reacted to the urgent need to escape. I turned and ran.

The trees grabbed at me, slapping wetly. Stones slipped beneath my feet. Wilhelm, who had been in the garden when Adrian told me. I could see the rectangle of light from the lounge. Footsteps pounded behind, getting closer. I could hear his heavy breathing. 'Oh, God, please help me. Ian! Ian!' My feet sank into a flower-bed. The shrubs held me. I fell, and a rose bush seemed to reach out, scratching my face. I scrambled up. Someone was silhouetted on the patio! Robert! I raced up the lawn and flung myself into the safety of Robert's arms, gasping for breath.

'Robert! Oh, Robert, thank heaven!'

I looked round, clinging to him. The moon had gone into a cloud. Wilhelm stood a few paces behind me, fighting to get his breath.

'He was there!' I gasped. 'At the zoo!'

189

Robert took me by the shoulders, his fingers pressing into me, and he said sorrowfully, 'Anne. Anne, I'm sorry. I didn't want this to happen. But you ...' He looked beyond me, at Wilhelm. 'What...'

'No choice,' Wilhelm said in a low voice. A horny hand, smelling of earth and nicotine, clamped over my mouth from behind. I tried to scream but no sound came and Robert stood there watching as Wilhelm's arm fastened round me like a steel bar.

'I'm sorry,' Robert repeated huskily. 'But you know too much. If you knew what was at stake ... We daren't risk ...' He went limp, like a relaxed marionette, his head bowed in an attitude of despair.

No, no! It couldn't be true! Kicking and struggling, to no avail, I was dragged away from the house. Robert! No, not Robert! I grabbed one of the shrubs, tears of terror running down my face. Wilhelm grunted and kicked at one of my ankles, jerking me away. Why, Robert? Why? My feet kicked up stones on the beach and I knew with perfect clarity that I was going to be drowned. It would look like suicide. Robert had skilfully implanted a doubt in everyone's mind about my sanity. Suicide while the balance of the mind...

The cold water of the lake lapped round my ankles. My last conscious thought, screamed silently and written in red neon across my mind, was one word—IAN!

CHAPTER ELEVEN

There were voices coming from above me. Beneath me, the ground was damp and my clothes were wet through. My hair stuck to my face.

Someone said, 'She's coming round.'

Opening my eyes, I looked straight into the anxious face of ... the refugee! Alan!

'Are you all right?' he asked.

People were coming from the house. I saw Ian push roughly past Bracke and the two policemen who were holding Robert and Wilhelm. He knelt down, lifting me into his arms, holding me very close and calling me his darling. All I knew was that I was safe. Ian was here.

'She's not badly hurt,' Alan said.

Ian looked up and I felt him start. 'Chas! Good God! Chas!'

I stared at the refugee. Chas? Ian's brother? Yes, there was a rightness about that. Contented, I drifted once again into oblivion.

CHAPTER TWELVE

The fire crackled and spat, throwing its
dancing light round the darkened room.
Outside, the wind howled round the old
Vicarage and freezing rain beat against the
window, while I sat curled on the hearth
rug, drifting along on the warmth and
security of my home. The aroma of baking
scones floated from the kitchen and
somewhere in the house my father would be
chewing the end of a pencil as he worked on
his sermon.

The firelight flickered on the Willow-
pattern dinner plates which adorned the old
oak dresser, as they had for as long as I
could remember. The velvet curtains were
new—I had helped Mother to make them.
Beside me, our old spaniel heaved a sigh of
contentment and buried his nose further in
his paws. I leaned over to scratch his ear
and as I did so Ian's last letter rustled in my
pocket.

I stared into the flames, seeing Ian's face,
hearing his voice speak the words of his
letter—'I can hardly wait to be with you.
There will be so much to say. I love you, my
darling.'

Dear Ian, I thought, smiling to myself. He
had looked so lost and lonely and he stood

waving on the tarmac when the plane taxied away, carrying Miriam and myself away from Berlin. We had left almost immediately after that last awful day, there being no need for us to stay. Ian had insisted that we should get away at once, but there were many questions left unanswered.

I knew that, despite my protests, Ian had told Bracke of our intention to confront Charles with the paper. The *Oberkommissar*, knowing that someone in the house was passing information, had agreed to leave it to Ian and hope that ensuing events would enable him to make an arrest.

Bracke himself had pulled me from the lake, while his fellow officers had captured Robert and Wilhelm. They had been taken away, and Ian and Alan had gone with them.

The following morning, at the quiet funeral which had been arranged for Adrian, I had seen Ian again, but no one had had much to say. It was decided that Miriam and I should leave on the evening flight. Like machines, we obeyed, our minds so numb with shock that we couldn't think, but I had wept to see Ian alone, receding to a tiny figure as the plane taxied away.

Miriam had been completely broken. White-lipped, she moved and spoke like an automaton. When I last saw her, she was being led away by an elderly gentleman who leaned heavily on a stick. Together they had left the airport terminal and driven away, out of my life for ever.

By some miracle of tact and discretion, the story had been kept out of the newspapers. There had been some short reports of Robert's death, from a heart attack, that autumn, in which literary critics briefly mourned the loss of 'a brilliant and gifted novelist'.

The spaniel sat up suddenly, one ear cocked.

'What is it, boy? What have you heard?'

A sharp knocking on the door answered my question. I sat still, my heart pounding, and heard the soft patter of Mother's feet come from the kitchen.

'Good evening,' said Ian's voice.

I leapt to my feet, startling the dog, who ran ahead of me into the hall and was jumping madly at Ian when I got there.

'Ian!' I cried, and launched myself at him, weeping with joy.

'I'm soaking,' he laughed eventually, and I noticed the wetness on his dark overcoat, the sprinkling of bright drops in his hair.

'Oh, darling, I'm sorry. Take your coat off and come and get warm. Mother, this is Ian.'

'So I gathered,' Mother said warmly, holding out a chubby, pink hand. 'Welcome home, Ian.'

'Thank you,' Ian said softly, and bent to kiss her cheek.

Mother's face glowed. 'You must be frozen. Go and sit down with Anne and I'll make you some cocoa.'

In the firelit living-room we sat on the ancient horse-hair sofa, holding each other close and whispering words of love. The spaniel flopped down on the hearth rug and went to sleep beside the steaming mugs of cocoa which Mother had brought.

'Did you tell your parents about it?' Ian asked eventually.

'No, I told them Robert was ill and didn't need me any more. When we heard that he was dead it seemed logical. They didn't need to know the truth.'

'I agree.'

'Why wouldn't you tell me anything in your letters?'

'I couldn't. At first I didn't understand anything myself, so there was nothing I could write that would have made sense. Afterwards, I didn't want to launch into long details. It was all too fresh to look at objectively. I wanted to tell you, when we were together, and once that's done let's forget it.'

'Yes, we will.'

'So where shall I start?'

'The refugee. Miriam told me he was

your other brother, but what was it all about? How did he get involved?'

'It all started through him. I told you his plane crashed ... well, he was over the Red Sea at the time and he baled out. The Russians naturally kept hold of him. He was reported dead, but Robert knew he wasn't. That's why he moved to Berlin. He was being coerced into passing information to them in return for Chas's life. It was easier in Berlin. Besides, Harry Smith was there.'

'Harry Smith?'

'Where do you think Robert got his information? It turned out that Robert had some hold over him for something that happened years ago, when they were both in the Army. I never did find out exactly what it was. But the Russians must have found out, somehow. They probably check everything like that.'

'But when Alan ... Chas escaped, why didn't he go straight to Robert and tell him? Why didn't he tell me?'

'For a start, he didn't escape. He was released. They'd just about wrung everything they could out of Harry, via Robert, so Chas was no use to them any more. But some joker took it on himself to let him loose in West Berlin, telling him that if he contacted Robert they'd kill them both. He was taken to the middle of the Havel, beaten up, and dropped overboard.'

'And I found him.'

'It was ironic, wasn't it? Like some deadly joke. You found him, hid him in Robert's house, and took him out of the city—using his own brother's passport. Nothing was said about how he left Berlin—Bracke decided to play that down, in view of what happened.

'Anyway, he got to Bonn and went to the Embassy, where he could be protected and arrange for a safety net around Robert, in case of trouble. They took some time proving his identity, but eventually he was flown back to Berlin and met Bracke. By the way, he sent you something.'

He reached into his pocket and drew out a small parcel which he gave to me with a smile. 'I think he envies me. He said this was part of the repayment he promised you.'

I opened the parcel. Inside was a box containing a silver locket in the shape of a heart.

'It's lovely,' I said, looking up at Ian. 'Shall we be seeing him again?'

'He's promised to come to the wedding.'

For a while there was only the crackling of flames and the beating of rain against the window as we drank our cocoa, but at last I put the mugs back on the hearth and settled again into the warm circle of Ian's arms.

'What about poor Adrian?' I asked.

'Yes,' Ian said grimly. 'Poor Adrian is right. He did hear a phone conversation— between Robert and Wilhelm, though Robert had nothing to do with the murder. Wilhelm took that on himself.'

'Where did he fit in?'

'He was Robert's contact man. And, of course, he heard what Adrian told you.'

Frowning, I said, 'That's been puzzling me. Wilhelm never understood English.'

'Of course he did. Don't you remember how, when we shot off to the zoo with Bracke, I asked him to tell Miriam where we were going? He understood that all right. We were fools not to notice at the time.'

'So he drove to the zoo and found Adrian before we did.'

'Minutes before. If he hadn't been hiding from us we might have saved him.'

'I wish he had told me everything,' I said quietly.

'If he had, you would have been dead, too. You came uncomfortably close to being killed as it was. It was Wilhelm you saw coming from the study. Robert had left those papers there for him to collect.'

'Robert,' I said in a low voice. 'I never considered him as a suspect ... Did you find out the truth about his accident? Was it Charles's fault?'

'No, it was Harry Smith. He deliberately bumped into Robert and bashed him with a ski. Unfortunately for him, he didn't hit hard enough ... Poor old Ellistone, all he ever did was make a vague promise to Miriam that he would try to copy some secrets. When that came out, he was dismissed from the Consulate.'

'It serves him right. I still hate him. Why did Robert ever put up with him?'

'I think he was genuinely sorry for Charles at first. Then when he saw what was developing he turned a blind eye to it, thinking that Charles would keep Miriam occupied, so she didn't enquire too closely into Robert's activities.

'That last night, as you've probably realised, Robert thought that Chas was still with the Russians. He was torn in two—not knowing how to save you and still protect Chas. But when Bracke got there Robert was trying to get you away from Wilhelm. He couldn't stand by and see you hurt. Whatever else he was, he was no murderer.'

'I'm so glad I know that,' I said softly. 'Poor Robert. He was in an impossible position.'

'Yes. He was. Harry Smith, of course, was court-martialled when the truth came out. It will be a long time before he and Wilhelm are free again.'

'It was a mess, wasn't it?'

'It was. But it's over now. Is there anything I haven't told you?'

'I don't think so.'

'Then please may we forget about it?'

Unnoticed, the fire sank to a glowing mound. The spaniel snuffled and sighed as he dreamed, while Ian lay on the old sofa with his head in my lap, his right hand holding mine tightly and his eyes closed.

A sudden thought occurred to me.

'Ian...'

'Mmmm?'

'I've just remembered something.'

'Good for you.'

I poked him in the ribs. 'Ian!'

'Yes?'

'I just remembered ... One day, while I was in Berlin, I saw Charles give *Frau* Decker something—a piece of paper, I think.'

'You saw who?'

'Charles Ellistone.'

'Oh, him!'

'Yes. He gave her something.'

'Gave who?'

'*Frau* Decker.'

'Who?'

'Heidi's mother.'

He looked up at me in the rosy dimness. 'What are you talking about?'

'One day, in Berlin, I saw Charles give *Frau* Decker something. And Heidi had said she was going to the East shortly afterwards. Do you suppose that Charles really was a spy, after all?'

Ian started laughing. Feigning annoyance, I pinched him very gently.

'Well, what do you think?' I demanded.

'My darling Anne,' Ian managed to say, 'we shall never know. And I'm certainly not going back to find out.' He sat up. 'Come here.'

'I thought you were nearly asleep.'

'I was, but I'm awake now. Are you resisting me again. I said...'